MW01593256

A Bottle of Glass Hearts

TABLE OF CONTENTS

Gem

No! Stop!

I'd have cried the words out loud but I held myself back. Not only could I be fired from any future job in the underground bunker without a warning, but it would mean I would distract Gem.

If I insisted that my anguished thoughts should be voiced for Gem's sake, there was no point to that either. His bright green eyes flicked to mine for an instant, and, even in the midst of his pain, he allowed a tiny smile to cross his small, boyish lips. To reassure me he was right where he wanted to be.

He was reading my thoughts.

I met Gemini last year back when I was Tuson Industries' excited new hire, bent on saving the world and doing great things for humanity. Over-eager to please, blond hair in a neat ponytail, and white blouse pressed and ironed, I, Soleil Punicello, was proud to call myself the youngest female to ever achieve the security clearance necessary to work for Tuson.

The mega corporation's sole purpose was to house, provide for, train, and assist the Omnicron – the child given the power to save the world.

The Omnicron was born with the magical gifts of telepathy, macro-teleknesis, genius intelligence, and, most importantly, the ability to hold the plates of our floundering planet together with his or her brain waves alone. Once the Omnicron died, usually at a young age in the line of duty saving the world, another would be born within the year to take their place.

Our planet, Topha, had suffered much destruction and was unstable. The land still sitting above water was wracked with quakes year after year, and the shallow core was riddled with holes and fault lines. A century ago, our people assumed we would all perish, land masses crumbling to bits and sinking under the oceans. We would collapse in on ourselves in one final great quake to end us all.

We spent years in prayer, begging our Lord God to save us from imminent extinction. And that's when the first Omnicron was sent, along with a vision to our prophets about her purpose. There have been six Omnicrons since then, Gemini being the current savior of our world.

Like most people, I always longed to meet the current Omnicron, knowing that he was a savior sent from God Himself to keep our planet alive yet again. The position was given the utmost respect, and the Omnicron was cared for like a right-hand angel to God Himself, or so I was told. Tuson Industries built an immense subterranean bunker. The complex was out of the public's eye but paid for by their eager donations and taxes. It was meant to house, protect, and get The Omnicron closer underground to the next chasmic Topha-quake. Unfortunately, the biggest quakes were always undetected by our surface scanners. Only the telepathic powers of the Omnicron himself could predict when he'd be needed to use the full capacity of his magical telekinesis to often literally rip his brain in half holding the planet together. Some Omnicrons survived their first core quake. Few survived two of them. They were always children. None lived longer than a decade or so. Until the next infant Omnicron was discovered, there was always months of panic among our people, wondering if the magic had run out, and if this current generation was going to be the one to witness the planet imploding.

When the next baby was discovered – and there was no rhyme or reason as to its origin of birth – he or she was given over to Tuson Industries to be raised by a staff of top security individuals who were equipped to train and educate someone of the Omnicron's intellect and talents. Knowing the child would also be able to read minds was another worthwhile reason to get him or her away from society as soon as possible.

Gemini, however, hadn't been discovered until he was already eleven years old. It was assumed that his parents had kept him a secret for over a decade, dooming the entire planet to wait in mass hysteria, thinking God had abandoned us once and for all. The risk his parents took hiding their son, hoping a core quake didn't slam the planet in the meantime, was an unthinkable abomination. When Gemini was finally discovered, after passing graduate school exams in the sixth grade, his parents were seized and imprisoned. Instead of the worldwide honor, prestige, and money they would have received, many said they received the death penalty. Others insisted they were handed a life sentence. Whatever the courts decided, it was hushed up, and they vanished into the abyss of the justice system, never to be heard from again. Gemini was an only child, so the officials could make his parents disappear and scare anyone from trying such an act in future generations.

I couldn't fathom what would make a couple choose their child over his righteous, God-given task. Yes, he would die, but he would've died if the planet's land masses all sank as well. Their brains must have been as foggy as my daily coffee – muddied with multiple heavy doses of cream. Their thinking was beyond selfish, and I had no patience for it. They were radicals. Self-centered lunatics so in love with their own son that they damned a planet of millions of people to its death.

But it also meant that Gemini had experienced real life outside of Tuson Industries. He was a genuine eleven-year-old boy when he came to live underground, and the powers-that-be were justly worried that he wouldn't take to his new life, would blame them for being separated from his parents, and would balk at his majestic future task.

Which all leads to me: Soleil Punicello. I was hired to be the Omnicron's personal secretary, aide, nanny, and mother-figure, in a sense. I was to "hang out" with the Omnicron, and meet his emotional needs in this transitional period.

I was thrilled. Having wanted to get into Tuson since my freshman year in college, I had taken classes in all the sciences, especially seismology, psychology, and childhood education. I was always at the very top of my class. I landed a government job straight out of college, and immediately worked on my security clearance. After writing a thick essay on my personal dedication to the Omnicron and the future of our planet, I was allowed to interview for the Omnicron's personal aid position, and landed the job at the tender age of twenty-four. Not only was the pay a sizeable raise due to the long shifts without a break, but the prestige and knowledge that I was making a mark on the world by emotionally, mentally, and physically assisting our most revered citizen was enough to let me die happy.

Badging in, stopping at a retina scanner, and pressing my palm to a screen that identified all five of my fingerprints, I was finally allowed to step inside the caged metal elevator that led down to Gemini's new home, and the giant lab at his disposal. Many countries were represented in the staff that worked underneath the ground – the Omnicron had united the world and brought about international peace – just one other thing that indebted us to him and his predecessors.

Clutching a tablet computer chock full of information pertaining to Gemini that I had read up on in the weeks prior to beginning my new job, I stepped out of the elevator. Glancing around at the sea green walls, I noticed they were all painted the same color – apparently a hue thought to be soothing and peaceful. It was better than white, to be sure, but still starkly naked and blank. This was no home for a child. This was like a military base.

The director, and head of Tuson Industries, stepped from around a corner, flanked by multiple guards. "Miss Punicello!" he called, pronouncing my name with an "s" sound instead of a "ch." "I'm Aster Glibson. Nice to meet you!"

I was slightly bothered that he had not done his homework on my name, musing that my role was supposedly of utmost importance to the Omnicron's mental health. Hiring someone like me was unusual in a unique situation of the corporation not having raised the child themselves. I would've thought I was valuable, and he would have done his research on me, like I had done on him.

I was taken around corridor after corridor, some lined with armed guards, until I arrived in a spacious schoolroom, outfitted with massive computer systems and an entire library of books. A child-sized but ample mahogany desk sat against the far wall, and there was Gemini. He had his back to the door and to us.

He was so small, so slight. His eleven-year-old shoulders were the size of boys his age, not broad enough to take on the weight of the world. His dark hair flopped over his forehead as he turned from the computer to look at us. His arms were thin, his chin boyish. He was so young.

"He likes to be called Gem," the director was explaining as Gemini stood up and turned around.

He fixed his gaze on me and stood stock still, staring me in the eyes for what seemed like an eternity.

"Remember," Aster Glibson murmured, "he can read minds."

Oh, I know. That was something I recalled – and feared – very clearly from my studies. I was desperately trying to wipe my brain of any thoughts, but all that kept going through my head was, *Oh my word, those eyes.*

Gem sighed.

I unpacked my bags in the sterile guest room I'd be sharing next to Gem's own large suite, suddenly worried that not seeing the sky for days on end would make me claustrophobic. I noticed the massive bottle of vitamin D pills in my personal adjoining bathroom, and the instructions, in my briefing, that I should not miss a day without popping two. I gulped. There had been so much information to take in at the initial meeting. My tablet computer now boasted a twenty page document of typed notes.

Gem studied for five hours a day, and practiced his abilities for another five. They had him on an aggressive schedule to compensate for the years of training he had missed. Everyone I met underground seemed on edge. Gem had only been living at Tuson for a month when I arrived, but he had done little to personally reassure anyone that he was capable of fulfilling his vital role. And, without knowing when the next core quake would hit, they had no idea whether or not he would be ready or willing to do his task. I surmised that most of his "education" involved emotional indoctrination and manipulation.

But he could read minds. He had to have known about his destiny all along. No one could keep a secret from him. *Why didn't he turn himself in?*

"Because I was protecting my parents."

I spun around. Gem stood at my open door. His gaze pinned me.

"What do you mean?" I asked. So much for get-to-know-you chitchat!

"No need for chitchat, Miss Punicello. I know you already." His voice was flat and matter-of-fact, as if patiently explaining a complicated concept to a child.

I said nothing.

"From almost birth, I had an understanding of what I was meant to do for the world. My parents were afraid because I was gifted, and they worried about whether or not I was the next Omnicron. They were really scared at the thought of giving me up, and my mom panicked inside every time she wondered about it. So I hid my magical gifts from the moment I was old enough to understand them. They didn't know. They weren't at fault."

"But... they were imprisoned –"

"They weren't. Instead of making The Savior Omnicron look selfish and deceitful, Tuson worked with the national justice system to pretend to 'do away with them,' but instead they helped my parents go into hiding. The world needed to make an example of them for show."

I sputtered. "What? Your poor parents! That's terrible! People are judging them falsely –"

Gem walked into my room and glanced at my small end table of personal items I had unpacked. He lifted my journal in his small hands.

"Don't –" I meant to stop him from opening it and reading it, knowing I had written all sorts of personal thoughts about his parents, him, my job, my future… But, in the instant I thought about it, I knew it was too late. He knew what I had written in that book as if he had read it himself. I lowered my gaze, ashamed.

20

He glanced at me, large green eyes thoughtful, sympathetic, yet piercing. "Miss Punicello, don't worry at all. Your thoughts are kind, innocent, and natural. Your mind is one of the cleanest I've met yet." He smiled at me, a look more of sadness than anything else.

I gaped and my face warmed. *Was that a compliment?*

"Yes." The corner of his mouth turned up for a second.

It hit me how much he must have suffered due to his telepathy alone. "You've seen and heard and experienced so much horror and evil by living out in the world and reading people's minds! You've been exposed to things no child – no human being – should ever be exposed to!" *Poor, poor precious boy. Your life is so unfair.* My throat went thick, and I shuddered.

Gem turned to face me, putting my journal back down on the table. His brows knit, and he spoke in boyish earnestness. "But you forget the other half of it. I also hear the amusing things that humans are too afraid to share. The weaknesses and vulnerabilities that people are afraid to expose to others." He gave me a pointed look. "Even you care about me already, and we just met."

My face grew hot. "I have cared about the Omnicron my whole life." My voice dropped to a whisper. "It's such a great honor to be here and help you."

Gem smoothed the front of my journal with his hand. "And just so you understand, I'll tell you something I didn't want to tell anyone else, because I don't care what they think of me." He stepped forward, voice lowered, "Even though I hid my gifts, I studied in secret. I always planned on stepping up to my role even from my own bedroom back in The States of Musi where I grew up. I would never have gotten out of my duty."

He spoke like an old man, his voice precise, measured, slow, and soft. There was no emotion in his words. He didn't even seem sadly resigned. Merely confident, calm, and assured.

He nodded – to my thoughts? "We understand each other now."

I smiled, hopeful. "Gem, you can just call me Soleil."

"Soleil, you walk, think, and even breathe loudly. Do you do that on purpose to be annoying?"

Gem was attempting to close all of the interior doors of the underground bunker with his mind simultaneously. It was a small macro-telekinesis task, and therefore challenging. Not being able to do micro-telekinesis meant he couldn't move small objects across the room, so shutting multiple doors in the base was difficult.

I was a distraction.

I often felt that I was completely unnecessary. Gem preferred to study alone. The silent thoughts he heard whenever anyone was in the vicinity were as loud as vocalized conversation would be to me.

"I'll leave!" I offered, packing up my tablet computer, in which I was doing my own research. I had purposed to get my masters degree in my spare time while I was stuck underground. There were many hours of the day where I sat in silence in my room, leaving Gem to study with his own quiet thoughts for a change.

"I didn't mean you should go," he insisted, his voice straining, eyes closed. His hands were clenched fists on the sides of his temple. "When I have to stop the next core Topha-quake, all of the staff and guards and directors and world leaders might be in the room. I'll have so many distractions. If I can't even close a bunch of doors with you right now, how will I save the world then?"

I was as silent as possible, focusing on emptying my mind for his sake, biting my lip as I watched his small forehead wrinkle and strain under the pressure. He stuck his tongue slightly out in concentration, and bunched up his nose. He was adorable.

He opened an eye at me. "Not helping," he said.

I blushed.

Finally, the door of the schoolroom slammed. And I heard the resounding noise of many doors down the hall shutting as well. They sounded like dominoes falling one after the other.

Two professors with clipboards bounded into the room, taking notes. "Excellent, Gemini!" one exclaimed, pushing his glasses up on his head.

The other scribbled furiously. "Take a break," he said to Gem, not looking up. He began murmuring to his partner and they left the room together.

Gem watched them go. He sighed, sinking into a chair at his desk, laying his head down on its surface. "They think I'm weak, and will never succeed."

I sat down next to him, wondering why I even bothered with the formality of conversation. "You should've spent some of your childhood years learning how to block out your telepathy for good!"

He was quiet for a time. "It's my sixth sense, in every way," he replied, eying me. "Just because you could hear ugly noises and insulting words, would you choose to deafen yourself permanently? Just because you could see something horrible, would you go blind on purpose?"

I blinked. "But it must get so loud and noisy... and awful!" I sputtered, looking for the right word.

"So I take a break and go be alone a lot." His high-pitched, prepubescent voice cracked a little. "But I'd still feel deaf or blind without it, no matter how much it's ruined me. At least it's nice to not have to hide it anymore."

"Ruined you?"

He pointed at me and lifted his head, not breaking eye contact. "You think I'm a hero – that I love this world and all of the people in it and am going to save them because I care so much. That's why *you* would save the world – if you were the Omnicron – because of love."

Of course he knew me better than I did myself. He could read the parts of my brain I hadn't acknowledged yet. "Wait, but –"

"I don't believe in love." Like a wise miniature sage, he lowered his gaze and shook his head solemnly.

I frowned, but stayed silent.

"It doesn't exist. And I don't think humanity is worth saving either. People are evil selfish cretins. Every one of them. Some just less than others. No one actually loves anyone more than they do themselves. Even my parents – who loved me most of all – had regrets about giving birth to me and raising me once in a while, and secretly hated and blamed me as much as they blamed themselves when I got taken away."

I was about to offer comfort and exclaim over him, when he held up a hand. "Oh, it doesn't hurt me in the slightest. I've never known any different or had any delusions about the way people really think."

Still. Hearing a child say it ripped my heart in two.

"This is hard for you to understand because your mind is purer than most." It was a line Gem had repeated a few times, matter-of-factly, as if to acknowledge that I was someone he approved of – and possibly pitied. I had come to treat it as the only compliment I was going to get from him.

A sudden sickening thought hit me. Instead of just letting him hear my thought on his own, I wanted to vocalize it and be given an answer. "Are you thinking of backing out? Of letting the world end?" This would be traitorous – complete treachery if anyone got wind of it. I hushed to a whisper and leaned close. "You would die anyway!"

He ruffled his floppy bangs and smoothed them back on his forehead. "I'll still do what I need to do. I'm the only one who can do it." Pride seemed to fill his face as he said it. "And I'll show them all what I'm mentally capable of. Besides, it's the right thing to do, and there really is no practical alternative. We all die, or I save the world, try to survive doing it, and then improve the world while I can. I don't plan on staying in this bunker my whole life like my predecessors." He turned to stare at me with earnestness. "In between quakes, if I live that long, I'm going to get a degree or two. I'm going to write scientific papers. I'm going to invent something. I'm going to do something else with my abilities! I'm not just going to prevent death, but I'm going to contribute further brilliance to the world."

Tears welled up in my eyes. His cheeks blushed pink as he read my thoughts, but he needed to hear them out loud anyway. "You are amazing. You are going to be the best Omnicron we've ever had."

"No one's thought *that* yet," he muttered, and his voice got thick. He looked down and played with his shirt hem, like a boy who is embarrassed, yet secretly pleased after being publicly praised by a doting mother.

"Your parents are going to be so proud. I'm proud of you already!" I cried, wishing with all my heart that I could hold him close and cradle him like the child he was.

He rolled his eyes at me and smirked. "Please don't." Then he rubbed his head. "I need a break from your overpowering gushy thoughts. I haven't done a single thing worthy of them yet." He stood up and walked out of the schoolroom without a backward glance.

It had been three months. We were in the playground area of our underground home. The walls in this particular space had been painted to look like blue skies and clouds with a bright UV light in the corner to represent the sun. I soaked up artificial vitamin D in a pool chair in the corner, sunglasses shading my eyes, but the farce pained me. Gem had experienced the vast expanse of a true sunny sky, and this was pathetic in comparison. The room was half the size of a football field, and boasted a gigantic playground, a full pool, and yard of grass. Fake or not, I had to admit that it was my favorite room. Gem hardly ever played in it, though, at

32

the mature age of eleven. But lounging in the attached hot tub helped his aching head and body after a hard day of telekinesis.

Today they were making him move the playground equipment in its entirety. He had to lift it up off the ground a full foot with his mind over and over again, like a grown man lifting weights. To teach him to keep his mind focused on the tiresome task even with distractions, they were having him answer mundane world trivia questions as he picked it up and dropped it. All in all, he had to lift the playground five hundred times by the end of the day. I hurt for him, even though he hated it when I had those kinds of thoughts. He liked it better when I went and stuffed my motherly mind into a good book inside of my lawn chair. Sometimes I sat at the top of the play equipment for fun, my added hundred and thirty pounds inconsequential. I'd root for him at the top while I enjoyed the little ride. It made the workout a bit more fun. At least, that's what I hoped. He seemed to appreciate when I acted like the kid he couldn't be. It made him laugh, which was nearly impossible for anyone else to do.

Today I flipped through "The Science of Planetary Plates" and tried not to let my mind drift. The two professors took notes as they quizzed Gem.

"Who led the Battle of Three Worlds?"

"Jerusha Galaxica," Gem replied with ease. "One hundred and twelve," he added, counting the playground lifts out loud.

"What was Topha's most mined resource back in 3010?"

"Clemzanite. One hundred and thirteen."

"Who were the parents of the first Omnicron?"

"Prophets Sola and Luna Farstar. One hundred and fourteen."

Gem's voice started to sound weary by the time he counted into the four hundreds. I had a bathing suit and a change of clothes waiting for him. The changing rooms stood behind me, and the hot tub was bubbling and ready. Placing my sunglasses on the small poolside table, I dragged my chair forward. I slipped my feet into the frothy water, shooting a guilty look at the trainers. I had done nothing to deserve the warm massage the jets were giving my toes. They ignored me, like usual.

"How many countries existed back in 1050?"

"Only sixteen." Gem took a deep breath. "And... five hundred!" His voice waned, and his shoulders slumped with the last thump of the gigantic playset.

The trainers, without a word of encouragement or backwards glance, began to chat among themselves and left the room. Gem dragged himself over to his bathing suit, picked it up, and headed to change. When he returned, he gingerly lowered himself into the water beside my feet.

I opened my mouth, but he beat me to my question. "It's not about getting praised."

"But..." I sputtered. "You did a great job. You answered every question right, and lifted five hundred reps with ease. I'm proud of you. Why don't –?"

"Who cares?" Gem bit his lip.

"There's something you're not telling me," I said, when he was silent and ignored my jabbing thoughts. "It's not fair when you do that. You can read *my* mind. Tell me yours."

My friendship with Gem was more than big sister-little brother. As the only human being able to read my mind and know me with that level of intimacy, I was as attached to him as one would be their right arm. He was like a second part of my brain by this point, and I could have studied him forever. He fascinated me and I dreaded losing him. I constantly threw away any thoughts of his dying whenever they tried to sneak up and stab me. I refused to think about it, hoping I successfully kept up an optimistic attitude for Gem in the process.

Just a week ago, one of the psychologists had approached me in the hallway, letting me know there was therapy and grief counseling they could offer me when Gem died. Angrily, I had told them it wouldn't be necessary, as Gem wasn't going anywhere, and I told them where they could stick their counseling services.

"They think I'll fail," Gem admitted, after a silence so long I had almost forgotten my original question. I sometimes wondered if Gem was forced to speak up just to silence my wandering brain when he ignored me. I'm sure my loud thoughts irritated him into speaking when he'd rather not. His head alone peeked above the water, and he glanced away nonchalantly, as if what he had just admitted was nothing.

"We've been over this before." I kicked gently at the cheerful bubbles.

"They think that my years without training means I'll fail. They think I'm going to die, and they're afraid I'm going to doom the planet in the process."

I went still. *So much pressure.* Literally the world on his childish shoulders. I felt myself go cold even as the hot steam wafted up to my face. "They do not."

Gem just looked at me, his big green eyes piercing. As if I could tell him he was wrong – when he read their minds every day.

I dropped my head and stared at the foam on the top of the water. "That's not fair. How can they think that? They treat you like a machine. No one down here cares about you at all! Don't they see how powerful and smart and strong you are?"

Gem smiled briefly, and I could tell I had pleased him with my last sentence. But then his mouth drooped once more. "Why should they care? They take on this job knowing I'm going to die. None of the professors or medical personnel or scientists or guards are the types to get attached. This is their job, and I'm a tool to save their world. And they think I'm going to die," he repeated.

Only two Omnicrons had survived their first core quakes, but none of them had failed in keeping the planet from breaking apart. Did everyone truly think Gem didn't have what it took? That he would fail when the other children had succeeded? Was I the only one who believed in him?

"You won't die!" I insisted.

"Not even I can know that. And I know everything." Even now, he was cracking a joke. He smirked at me, but his face held more sadness than mirth.

I got off my chair, crouched down, and reached for his hand, which lay across the top Jacuzzi step. "Gem, you have to believe that you're not going to die. You've got to have a will to live. You've got to will your body to survive that quake, and to not give up while you give it your all. There's power in having a positive attitude in the midst of danger!"

He cocked an eyebrow at me, but didn't withdraw his hand like I had expected. It lay limp in mine, but he didn't take it back. "Will to live? Nothing scientific about that, Soleil. I don't believe in things I can't measure scientifically. They're probably right, and I'll die."

Desperation hit my mind in a panic, and it reached Gem. He finally yanked his hand out from beneath mine and sunk below the surface of the water in a hurry, his head disappearing underneath the bubbles. For as long as he could stay under, he would be free from my thoughts. I used that time to hurriedly run through a gamut of things I could say to argue with him. Wracking my brain for what to use, I sat back down on the pool chair.

Before I could come up with an answer, he reappeared, only his eyes and nose showing above the surface. He glared at me. Then, sputtering, he popped completely out of the water and turned his back to me. "Back when I was in third grade, there was a boy in my class who came down with a rare disease."

A friend? I listened intently, clearing my mind of my own thoughts, straining to hear his soft words.

Gem craned his neck back to look at me over his shoulder and rolled his eyes. "I don't have any friends." He snorted. "Why would I? Especially other children? They're juvenile. Selfish. Stupid. I didn't have any patience for them ever. And they all either hated me or I totally scared them. I could read their minds, remember?"

I bit back a retort and stayed quiet.

Gem sighed. "This kid was kind of different. He didn't just know God existed, like the rest of us, but he had a relationship with Him. He loved God and had faith in His goodness – something I had never believed in – because of how crummy my own future looked."

I felt tears prick in my eyes but focused on repeating the words Gem had just said in my mind – a trick I used to shut down my own thoughts.

Gem could read my emotions though. He splashed the water with a fist. "He was going to die. The chances of him surviving that disease were slim. But the doctors told his family, 'If he has a will to live, he can survive this surgery.' I read his mind. He wanted to live *badly*."

I jumped in. I couldn't help myself. "The same thing happened to a girl in my class in high school! And she made it! See, Gem? She made it! And so can you!"

Gem ignored me, calmly rising out of the Jacuzzi and reaching for his towel. He dried himself off without saying a word. Finally, he threw the towel back down on the chair and grabbed his clothes. "Well, the boy in my class *died*, Soleil. Will or no will, he *died.* At least he was going straight to the God he loved so much. I'm supposed to save the world, but I couldn't save him, Soleil. I couldn't even save the one person I could actually tolerate. I'm not going to be able to save *anybody*!"

The night I finally had an idea, I knocked frantically on Gem's door far past bedtime. He opened it, and I could see he wasn't in bed or even in his pajamas, but dressed in a soft gray martial arts-like outfit. The loose cotton clothes – Gem's choice – had been saved for one purpose: the day of the core quake.

My heart plummeted. "Why are you wearing that?"

"It's time, Soleil. I haven't woken everyone up yet. But I can feel it. It's going to happen in the next couple of hours. I'm just getting myself calmed down and ready before everyone goes crazy."

He was talking nervously and quickly, but his words blurred in my ears. A rush of shaky, chilly panic blocked my ability to hear him. *No.* This couldn't be happening. He wasn't going to suffer tonight! The world wasn't going to end tonight. A blinding panic over my own possible death hit me in the gut, but I shook it off as quickly as it came. I wasn't going to die, nor was I going to lose Gem. Not now! Not ever!

I took him by the shoulders. "Look, Gem. Maybe it's me. Maybe if I just believe hard enough *for* you, you'll survive. That's my job, right? I'm your encouragement and support. I believe in a God who loves you. I'll will you to save this stupid world and live!"

Gem stood still and silent. Varying looks of fear, desperation, and pity for me crossed his face. When he spoke, it sounded weak and shaky. "What've I got to lose?" His voice caught on the last word, and he took a deep breath. "Time to go."

My breathing picked up. Should I throw my arms around him? Give him a last benediction? He can't just leave! He could be going to his death! *No! I'm one who will never stop believing he can survive this!*

Reading my thoughts, he cut me off. "So there should be no fanfare then. I'll see you after this is over." He bravely smiled. His chin quivered, but he jerked his shoulders out from under my hands and marched away.

I stifled a sob and followed.

The news went out quickly on the radio and emergency sirens. Get to the safe houses all over the world. Start praying. This was the big one.

They set Gem up in a partly reclined, Frankenstein's monster-like chair with straps for his arms and legs, a pillowed section for his head, and soft classical music of his choice playing in the background.

"Let us know if you want the sound turned off or the lights dimmed," a nurse said.

There was a frantic energy in the room, even though all of the personnel were organized in doing their jobs. Director Glibson himself strapped Gem down onto the chair and started an IV. "If you're sure you can feel the beginning tremors, then we'll get you ready. Like we've told you before, we can't give you pain medicine because it will interfere with your telekinesis signals and concentration. I'm sorry. But the drugs going through the

IV will keep you from passing out," the director murmured, but I heard it, perched by his side. "Miss Punicello," Glibson turned to me next, "we need everyone back at the far end of the room out of the Omnicron's way and into the adjoining safe area where you'll be protected from the quake."

The safe area was just a side wing of the main lab where Gem sat. We were strapped down with five point harnesses to seats built into the wall. The whole lab was like a fortified castle, impenetrable and all one large piece of seamless steel. It would protect us from other parts of the bunker caving in. Nothing had been destroyed in previous core quakes, however, due to the nature of the bunker's foundations. They were built on moving springs and padded cylinders, wrapped in layers of rubber and steel. The whole facility shifted with the quake, as long as the Omnicron did their job and kept the worst tremors at bay. I knew Gem preferred they'd all leave entirely so he wouldn't have to hear their terrified thoughts screaming at him, but there was nowhere else but this room that could ensure our safety.

His eyes searched mine for an instant as I left. I pumped my fist in the air at him and swallowed hard. *I'm fighting for you, Gem. You can do it. Stay alive. You are strong enough. I believe you can do this. God chose you and loves you, Gem!*

I knew he heard my thoughts, but he heard everyone else's too. Hopefully mine were the loudest. He turned his head away and stared at the ceiling.

And then it began.

Gem's body tensed, his arms straining against the straps. He grunted once and then relaxed.

"Are you okay?" I called before thinking.

A dozen stern voices shushed me.

"It's starting, Soleil. It's not too painful yet. I can feel the center of Topha!" Gem answered me, as if we were the only two people in the room, as if to spite those who silenced me. He sounded awed and excited.

My heart warmed. I sent a smug look back at everyone else. *He'll exceed all of your measly expectations. You just wait and see. You may know his brain and his body's capabilities, but you don't know his heart and soul and strength like I do. You're idiots. All of you.*

The waves of tension came and went for an hour, Gem tensing and breathing heavily for a few minutes each time. And then it hit full force. The ground shook, and all of us clutched our harnesses and rode it out. Gem's eyes closed and his hands clenched and unclenched. The veins in his head and neck throbbed, and his breathing became frantic. He fought hard, grinding his teeth. It hit me in the gut: he was literally holding the world together.

Tears silently poured down my cheeks. *You can do it, Gem! You were made for this!* My thoughts screamed in my head at him. *Stay alive for me, Gem! Do it for me!*

Sweat pouring down his boyish face, Gem turned his head toward me. It was the first time in two hours he had acknowledged anyone in the room. But now he looked me right in the eyes. Everyone bent forward, straining to listen over the roaring of the world. Panting hard, and clearly in tremendous pain, Gem managed to smirk. "Will someone tell the egotistical blonde that I'm not saving the world for her sake alone?"

A few people let out nervous chuckles. The tension dissipated. Tears of embarrassment and relief flooded my face. *Oh, you smart aleck. You're going to be okay. You're going to be okay!*

But the next hour was sheer hell. The ground bucked beneath us. Gem's agony intensified. He writhed and twisted in his restraints, wailing and moaning. They kept him from lapsing into unconsciousness with the constant trickle of adrenaline drugs through his IV. Blood leaked out of his nose and ears, and I could see that he had chafed a line of raw skin straight through his socks around his ankles every time he bucked in his restraints.

I wanted to turn and run, to flee the possibility that I was watching the death of the little boy who had become the dearest person to me. But I dared not leave. I would give him the honor of watching his struggle, shouting my thoughts into his shell-shocked mind, staying by his side at all times, and witnessing the greatest act of heroism I had ever seen from a human being, let alone a child. He was saving the lives of all of the millions of people on our planet. That blood leaking from his nose and ears was the most beautiful thing I had ever seen. The marks on his hands and feet. The veins in his neck. The air rasping raggedly from his lungs.

In all of my life, I would never forget this moment. This was bravery. This was love.

And then the shaking went still. Gem's body slumped. His lungs slowed down. His hands and face went limp. It was over. We were saved.

For the next two weeks, it was touch and go. Gem had survived the core quake, barely, but his body was in shock. He lay in a coma for what seemed like an eternity, nurses and doctors bustling around checking his vitals every hour. Tubes ran in and out of his nose and mouth, needles in his arms. I sat by his bedside almost every waking moment, leaving only to sleep in my room at night, praying on my knees that he would survive.

They told me that even if he did wake up from his coma, his brain could be vegetative. He could be deaf or blind. He could be paralyzed. The doctors and professors and guards I had thought so unfeeling helped me keep constant watch over him, their faces finally showing their deep concern, their fears, and their immense gratitude. Suddenly we were one family, all praying and waiting for Gem.

And then, after the two longest weeks of my life, a nurse ran to get me in the middle of the night, the sound of her knock frantic on my door. I jumped out of bed, grabbed my bathrobe, and ran to the infirmary. And there he sat, weak but upright, and very much alive. His eyes, huge in his thin face, held all of the same luster from before, and I could see the fathoms of intellect behind them.

He was going to be okay.

Gem held out his arms, and I hugged him as tightly as I dared. When I tried to back away, he continued to hold me, and that's when I began to bawl, clutching him back as all of my fears fell out onto my cheeks in rivers of tears.

"You were right all along, Soleil," Gem whispered, almost too soft to catch.

"Wasn't I?" I sobbed and scolded. "You're alive! Just maybe God really gives us things we can't measure. Emotions, love... faith! Maybe I had the answers all along, and the Know-It-All had to learn that from someone far stupider than himself!" I sniffled and laughed all at once.

For a long minute, Gem was silent, his face stuffed into my shoulder, and then he took a deep breath. He pulled back and looked me in the face. "You were right, Soleil," he repeated. "There's so much I still don't know. And I'm so ready to get out there and find out. My life isn't over yet. We've got a lot to do together! No more giving up." He looked at me with a smile illuminating his tear-stained eyes.

I couldn't wait to begin.

His Bottles of Tears

"Please! Don't hang up on me! I want you to come home!"

My cry echoed hollowly as the dial tone stung my ear. Dropping the receiver, the burning hit my eyes with a hellish fervor. They stung until the saltwater tears poured out to douse the fire behind my vision.

She wasn't coming home. My beautiful, lovely, one and only teenage daughter. Lost to me, she refused to leave the sin and return. Repenting and begging for forgiveness wasn't on her rebellious bucket list.

Was this the fifth time I wept today? The constant falling of life-water onto my face did nothing to assuage my heart. Like a bandage that would not stick, the tears failed me, but still, they would not cease.

Drained with grief, I stumbled back into the room where my husband lay sleeping, and crawled under the heavy quilt. Wrapping myself securely, I crouched near his warm body, trembling with the shivering sobs. Chill seeped in through the sheets. Would I ever be able to set a firm chin of resignation to this issue of my precious baby daughter?

Within seconds of forcing my eyelids to clamp a lid on the sorrowful leaking from behind my eyes, I found myself opening them once again inside a bright white room. Jars and bottles of all shapes and sizes stood shoulder to shoulder like ardent glass soldiers in strict formation. They occupied every inch of hundreds of rows of shelves affixed to the wall, and held transparent, sparkling liquid up to their brims. The room was radiant, unseen lights reflecting off of the white walls and the crystal clear bottles.

I did not hear Him arrive, but there He stood beside me. He stretched out His hand to me, his robe as pristine as the room, the white soft on my swollen eyes.

"Where are we, Lord?" I worried. Had my heart finally cracked beyond repair and given up the fight? Was this Glory? Then why did I still feel so heavily unhappy? What was this absence of peace, even as I stood in Jesus' presence?

"These are my treasures," He said softly, His voice soothing my ears like feathers against the cheek. "Each of these hold the tears of my children."

With a gasp, I surveyed the room again, staring at the precious life-water of my brothers and sisters. Some jars were larger than milk jugs, holding gallons of sorrow in their bellies. They could only represent numerous days and nights of ripped hearts and tortured souls.

Thinking of my own impossible battle with my daughter, of the messy breakup that had destroyed my college years, and of the miscarriage I once faced as a newlywed, I suspected my own bottle was fairly immense.

Turning doe eyes to my Lord, I enquired, "Where is mine?"

With a strong finger, He pointed to the corner shelf, second from the bottom.

There sat a miniature vase, its thin neck holding no more than a pint of the clear salty tears I had donated over the years. I stared in disbelief. "Are you sure you didn't miss any, Lord?"

"I miss nothing." There was a sweet smile on Jesus' lips.

In an instant, I forgot about my own miniscule bottle, and straightened up, gazing about the room again in horror. Striding purposefully over to a vessel the size of a small aquarium, I tapped its face with my fingernail. "What happened to him?" I demanded, dread filling the gaps between my lungs and ribcage.

Jesus' eyes melted with a wise sadness that was married to joy and hope, a look of which my own timid faith could not mimic if I tried. The corners of my eyes were far too wrinkled with doubt to attempt it. "His entire village was murdered at the hands of radical militants. They burned down his church, leaving him crippled. His whole family was killed, and his wife died in his arms."

With a gasp of pain, my hand reached for the great big jug of tears, and brushed back and forth against the glass as if I could wipe them away forever. I felt useless and helpless and my own sorrows fled. "Why?" I whispered, eyes shut.

"He travels to all of the surrounding nations, giving his testimony and leading many to Me. He is writing a book that will bring thousands to Me. His entire church and family rest in my Father's bosom in heaven awaiting his coming to join them for eternity."

I stepped a few paces to the right and found another. Large, intimidating, and sloshing with fresh tears. "And her?"

"She was sexually abused by her father for ten years. It began at the age of four and didn't end until she ran away with her mother as a teenager, living on the streets and eating out of trashcans."

"And...?" I waited, my heart racing in agony.

Jesus took my hand. "And she has started a nationwide ministry that provides shelter and education for abused women and their children. Every day she frees hundreds of lives."

Encouraged and emboldened, I found yet another giant bottle, the tears of which were almost overflowing.

"She has multiple sclerosis and hurts every single day. Her husband left her, her family has all abandoned her, and she is completely alone, trapped in her own failing body."

I knew what to expect this time. Jesus would tell me why. There was a happy ending to this story too.

"She came to know Me. She loves Me better," He said simply.

"No extravagant ministry or worldwide fame?" I asked, hesitating.

"No one knows her name," Jesus replied. "But it is enough that it brings her soul daily into my arms."

I pointed to my own tiny vase once more. "Why have I not suffered like these? Why have I been spared so much mourning? Why have you given me an easy life in comparison?"

"Because, My dear child, it would not have glorified Me or been for your best to give you more. What you have now is good for you. You bring honor to Me in your responses, and I see and hold your fewer tears just as close to my heart. They are precious jewels in my sight, and more valuable to me than gold. You have been a good and faithful servant with what I have allowed you."

All of me resonated with His words, as they spun through my head and radiated out my fingertips and my toes. My body felt light, and the peace I longed for coated my limbs. All I could control in that moment was my knees, which dropped to a deep kneel at His feet.

He moved away from me, reaching for my own vase. In His other scarred palm, He held a new, slightly larger bottle. With deft hands, He poured my tears into this bigger vessel, discarding the old.

In an instant, the supernatural peace fled from my immature, unstable mind. His words disappeared, my flimsy brain forgetting them. All I could see was the greater bottle, glaring at me with its smooth surface. My tears only occupied two thirds of its inside, ominously prophesying of weeping that was to come.

"What are you doing?" I demanded, rising to my feet, my hands clenched. "Are you implying I will be crying so much more soon? I thought it wasn't for my good! I thought I was good enough now!" My spirit cried out silently that my words were vain and foolish, and not fit to be spoken in front of my King, but I did not heed this warning. I was consumed with unreasonable fear.

His kind face remained unchanged. With the same look of compassion, He took my hands in His once more. "My daughter, there is no inherent goodness within yourself. And d d you forget so quickly what I did in the lives of My other children? Do you still not trust Me?"

Biting my lip, I shushed my mouth and hung my head. "Help me!" I murmured. "Because it is so very hard. It should not be, but yet it is!"

The doorbell roused me from sleep and I was once again huddled against the strong back of my husband, our familiar bedroom walls alerting me that it had been a dream. The incessant chiming cried to be noticed. Who could it be so early? The sun had only just begun to apply blush to the cheeks of the sky. I pulled on the knob and swung open the heavy front door.

There she stood. My lovely, broken, weeping daughter. Her cheeks were pale, her makeup smudged. But her lowered, shamed eyes were clear. She lifted them to me and fell into my outstretched arms. "Mama, I'm home!"

Again, the saltwater cleansed my cheeks. These were the new tears of which He had hinted. Tears I had been afraid to meet. I knew they would flow for hours.

Tears of *joy*.

Curls for Rae

He began to notice her by the third week. She arrived every Wednesday night, promptly at five pm, an hour before closing. Her lightly tanned skin looked paler and paler each time, and her mouth slumped more and more into a wearied frown. Soft doe-like brown eyes hid behind long lush lashes, eyelids always downcast. Her gaze rested on the floor or beyond his shoulder every time he tried to make eye contact with her. She didn't look anyone in the eye. She was young – still in her twenties – but sadness lines seemed permanently etched on her forehead.

But her hair!

Waves of the most velvety-looking brown tresses, thick in volume but fine of strand. The curves of it followed the narrow edge of her face and chin, landing to pillow on small shoulders, caressing her upper arms like an embrace.

Blaine York knew hair. It was part of his job description.

Partnering at "Upper Cuts," a downtown salon and boutique, Blaine cut hair for a living.

He tapped the faucet handle, and the sudden silence filled the room. Closing time after a busy mid-week day. Blaine watched the water swirl down the drain, chasing itself to the dark sanctuary of the pipes. One final drop lingered around the shiny chrome at the bottom. He stared at the warped reflection of his nose, his reverie only broken by his ears picking up the sound of his hairdresser partner closing up the cash register.

Blaine reached for the downy white towel hanging next to the sink and thoroughly dried his hands before turning around. "Marguerite," he called to the other stylist, "your last customer – who was she?"

Marguerite's vivid yellow-bleached spikes swayed as she propped her right elbow on the counter, her left hand jotting notes in a thick ledger. "Looks like..." She glanced over. "...the clipboard said her name's Rae."

"With an 'e' or a 'y'?" Blaine asked. Somehow it was important.

"E."

He exhaled. Of course. It was the only way to spell it on a woman. The rich reds and greens of the name painted a picture in his mind. Rae. Solemn Rae with the luscious World War II era tresses. Hair the color of the brown sugar cinnamon topping his mother always dumped lavishly on her sweet potato casserole at Christmastime.

"Do you know her?" Marguerite cracked her gum, making Blaine flinch. He hated the intrusively noisy habit, but heard it cut her cigarette needs down to one or two a day. She was trying to quit – the least he could do was be sensitive and understanding.

"No," he said simply, and then felt the need to explain. "She's come in like three weeks in a row, I think." Hadn't she been satisfied with Marguerite's job the last two visits?

A crease popped up on Marguerite's vampire-white forehead. "She hasn't complained about my work," she murmured, as if reading Blaine's mind.

He hesitated in his steps toward the back room. "Want me to take her if she comes in again?"

His partner chuckled. "Is that your way of saying you want a chance with her?"

Blaine's cheeks warmed but he shrugged and laughed it off. "She's got good locks." He turned to peek at Marguerite over his shoulder. "What's she been getting when she comes in?"

The hairdresser bit down on the tip of her pencil and leaned both elbows backward on the counter. "Hmmm... a light feathering and small trim. Half-inch at most."

Was Rae cautious, wanting to chop it off but afraid to do more than the smallest smidgen at a time?

Marguerite grinned. She wagged her pencil at him. "Maybe she has a hot date every Wednesday night and wants her hair just perfect for it, but she's embarrassed to simply ask for styling."

Blaine was unhappy at the thought, and the feeling didn't surprise him. When a woman caught his eye and intrigued him – which was rare – he hoped she was exclusively single. Not that he had dated much, even though many of his clients seemed embarrassingly enamored with him. Twenty-five years old, male, single, and not gay? He knew how rare that was to find in the industry. But he was waiting for the woman – and the hair – that would speak right to his heart. And he hadn't found her... yet.

"Marg, no one that sad would have a hot date, don't you think?" He spun on his polished leather heels and headed for the back room to gather his bag.

"You're right. She had quite a puppy-dog look about her, didn't she?"

"More like someone killed her puppy dog," Blaine called over his shoulder. The swinging back door shut behind him, and he picked his way around the cluttered chairs, grocery bags, and empty water bottles that littered the breakroom. Marguerite might keep an immaculate shop, but the backroom was her best kept secret that hid her real disorganized personality. He'd probably have to be the one to pay the rent again this month and bill her later. At least she had agreed to keep a more accurate ledger.

A tumble of donuts sat in a greasy pink cardboard box on the plastic table in the center of the room. Nothing would entice Blaine's refined tastes to take one, so he firmly closed the lid in a last-ditch effort to keep the remains from going stale. The sugary yeasty smell the box gave off reminded him of his mother, and he closed his eyes for a second to imagine her cooking homemade donuts at Easter.

Thoughts of Blaine's mother always came with thoughts of his stiff, traditional father, his serious lips a constant thin line. It was as if James T. York always feared originality and spontaneity would burst out and humiliate him one day, so he kept his thoughts firmly tied in the back of his throat. Growing up, it was hard to get the man to say more than three sentences a day, and they tended to be always the same like a stuck old-fashioned record: "Thank you for the coffee" (always black), "Supper was delicious, my dear," (always after having finished his entire plate), and "How was school, Blaine?" (to which "Okay, Dad" was always the answer).

Blaine's mother had named him – the woman was bursting with creativity that was slowly and lovingly stifled under her husband's stick-in-the-mud monotony. So she cooked. Baked. Broiled. And sautéed. And she was pretty darn good at it too. Her confections could have won her a spot in a top bakery. But those masterpieces were created for the York family mouths only, to Blaine's dismay.

The day he had announced he wanted to be a hairdresser, his mother's eyes had sparkled without surprise. He had been playing with her graying wiry strands since they were blond and springy. He had kept her looking glamorous for years.

But his father's eyes had blinked in horror. "Isn't that a job for women?" had been the expected dark-ages reply from James T. York, banker and owner of three navy blue suits and two gray ties.

"I'm an artist, dad. It's an art. And I really love people." Blaine threw out a chuckle as if he didn't care. But he did. Confrontation wasn't his strong suit, and he wanted the fight to be over before it began. "I already have enough for school and you don't have to spend a cent."

Blaine had kissed his mother's wet cheeks, moved out, and a thousand practice hours and a license later, teamed up with Marguerite, a schoolmate. She had a steady military boyfriend and an inheritance from a beloved grandmother, and so she offered him a partnership strings-free. At that point, even James T. York saw Blaine was committed. The day his father came in to Upper Cuts for his standard Ivy League cut was the day Blaine felt he had arrived.

"Did you take a donut?" Marguerite asked as Blaine walked past her, keys jangling, messenger bag thrown over one shoulder.

He tugged on a rolled up shirt sleeve and reached for his plaid blazer. "No, thanks, Marg. Remember to pay the rent, okay?"

He waited for her in growing anticipation all that next Wednesday.

She's not going to come. The third haircut was the charm. Who comes in four weeks in a row for the same little trim? She's not going to come. The words drummed through his skull like a ruler on his knuckles, attempting to beat his unwilling hope into an early death. But he always found this particular emotion hard to kill, and he found himself twitching and glancing at the door every two minutes as it got closer to early evening. At one point he noticed it had begun to rain, but still she hadn't come.

Blaine was deep in conversation with old Mrs. Grauwer, dyeing her hair a new shade of burnt rose, and hearing about her granddaughters' prowess as a Girl Scout, when Marguerite's voice called out sharply, "York." It was the tone she only used for him, and his brain was tuned to pick it up over the usual chatter and Indie rock echoing throughout the salon.

He set down the last strip of aluminum foil and turned to make eye contact with his partner. She nodded her head in the direction of the door.

Rae.

Her full lips set in a frown, her eyebrows slanted upward, she carried that same foggy aura of depression around her like a robe. Her shoulders sagged under her camel-colored raincoat, and her black ballet flats were trailed by a little shadow of wet, marking her presence on the sparkly tiled floor.

Blaine's heart gave a little leap of happiness, and his mouth turned up at the corners. "Can I have her?" he mouthed to Marguerite, but the spiky-haired beautician had already turned back to her client. "I'll be right back, Mrs. Grauwer." Blaine met eyes with the elderly woman and relaxed into a large smile.

"Don't worry, young man!" she chirped.

Blaine practically waltzed over to the young woman waiting. "Rae, right? We were expecting you again today!" Was that too forward?

Like a timid baby rabbit, Rae visibly winced. She shrunk inside her deep, furry hood, her eyes only flicking up to meet his for the briefest of seconds. "Thanks. You have a good memory."

"Were you hoping for Marguerite again this week? I'm available in just a minute." *Please...*

She shook her head. "No, that's fine." Her golden eyelashes lowered, and she played with the shoulder strap on her purse, staring at her shoes.

Blaine bit his lower lip. He was great at keeping a conversation going with his clients, but not very skilled at starting one. He preferred to listen and ask questions. Could he make this shy but lovely young woman feel comfortable?

After getting Mrs. Grauwer situated under the dryer chair, he forced himself to walk smoothly and calmly back to Rae who was perched on the edge of a shiny plush chair by the entrance, staring out at the falling rain.

"Can I take your coat?" Blaine asked. He helped her quietly shrug out of the raincoat, and hung it on an old-fashioned coat rack by the door, right next to his own blazer.

He led her to his salon chair and adjusted the height by the foot petal. She was shorter than Mrs. Grauwer by a little bit.

Her hair cascaded around her shoulders in smooth waves, still buttery brown with a hint of cinnamon. She looked like a pin-up picture of a 1940s Broadway star. He grinned. Her hair and face were a work of art, just like her name. "What can I do you for?" he said, voice chipper and playful, slipping into vintage lingo.

She stared at his reflection above her in the mirror. "C-can…" she began softly.

Blaine leaned his head down to hover next to hers, staring straight ahead at her through the mirror's surface. "What was that?"

"Can you make me look like a celebrity?" she asked. She blushed and her chin quivered.

In a heartbeat, Blaine could see that she wasn't just timid. This wasn't shyness. It was a deep sorrow. The aura around her face changed to one of such deep blue. Her full lips trembled, her hands on the armrests shook, and her slim neck muscles worked as she swallowed rapidly. He took this all in at a glance.

"Miss Rae," he said, wishing for all the world that he was wearing his grey fedora that day so he could tip it, "making you into a celebrity would be my honor." He gave a small sweeping bow. "And the easiest thing I'll have to do all day," he added.

The color rose in her cheeks. "I don't deserve that..." Her voice broke on the last word and she looked up at the ceiling quickly as if to stop tears. She took a deep breath and said, "Thank you..."

"Blaine. I'm Blaine." And then he reached out for her hair.

Like he did with all of his clients, he let the feel of it overwhelm his senses. He held it in his hands and simply waited. There it was – the memory came tiptoeing into his mind. The touch of Rae's hair reminded him of the softest quilts his grandmother made, all downy and velvet. Light as a feather, yet thick enough to hold back the dew on the summer mornings when he'd lie out on the lawn with her and watch the sunrise. Summers as a small boy at Grandmother's in the country. Fluffy pink quilts. Scones for breakfast with chocolate milk.

Blaine closed his eyes as he ran his fingers through Rae's hair. This was how the magic happened – when he tapped into a synesthetic memory that fit his client's specific tresses. To understand the soul behind the hair. And then he worked, often feverishly, to create the masterpiece in his mind's eye.

Rae needed so little done. She was as close to satisfactory as a client ever was. However, if he layered a little, cut some wispy side bangs, and curled everything with a large barrel iron, he could see her now – she'd be an angel. Satiny locks of cupid perfection. Bring her aura from depressed blue to shining gold. She'd be his muse for all time.

More excited than he'd been in a long time – having just been given free reign for his own hyper creativity, he stuck his tongue out through his lips, seized his favorite scissors and a sterilized black comb, and began. Drowning his mind in the tunes of Moby wafting lazily and nostalgically through his shop, he plunged his mind into focus, and flung his fingers back into her hair.

Senses on high alert, Blaine was a whirlwind, hands everywhere. He stroked her forehead, coaxing the new bangs to lie exactly where he placed them. Blowing lightly on the back of her neck, he wiped her soft tan skin clear of clippings. Cupping her ear, he protected it from the careful sweep of the comb as it loosed the new curls into a lighthearted bounce.

Every once in a while, he would catch her eyes watching him through the mirror under those long lashes. He gave her just quick glances, without acknowledging her stare, but the thought of her look spurred his resolve to complete his masterpiece without flaw. She was his in that moment. His darling. He was the master of her fate. He would improve her life, just a little bit. Hairdressing was a work of love. A betterment of humanity. He felt it in his aching heart. *Be happy*, every clip of his scissors whispered to her. *Be happy. You are beautiful. You are worth this.*

At one point, near the end, when he was untangling a final curl gently with his fingers, he caught the sound of a sniffle, a tiny gasp of breath, felt a quickened pulse at the side of her neck where his thumb rested.

Dropping the curl as if it had burned him, he backed up, terrified, to see why she was upset. "Oh, I'm sorry, Rae!" he blurted with a reflexive uneasy chuckle. "Did I do something wrong?"

Silent tears streamed down her cheeks, little glittery beads following one after another in an orderly line. Free-flowing, they brazenly exposed her heart with every bold new drop.

Frozen in place, Blaine dropped his hands in horror, one hitting the side of the chair with a painful crash. "Ouch," he muttered.

Rae shook her head, large curls floating with her. "It's perfect," she whispered. She brutally swiped a hand across her eyes. "Sorry. It's nothing."

Blaine's shoulders sagged with sudden relief, and then quickly straightened again as wonder followed the emotion. As he reached to undo the barber's cloth snapped tightly to her neck, he felt his spine stiffen with pride and excitement. Was a client truly crying over his work? Had his muse proved as wonderful as he had hoped? This was a day he would never forget.

"I'm glad." Two simple words that didn't convey a tenth of what he really wanted to say. He grinned all lopsided, cocked his head, and rubbed the back of the buzzed lower half of his hair. He then pulled on his longer top locks and cleared his throat. "You are gorgeous."

She shook her head again, sinking her gaze back to the floor, the spell broken. "That's only because I look like Maura now."

It would be intrusive to enquire which celebrity Maura was – who she had been trying to emulate. He also lacked the courage to argue with a client, and he had no words to describe how immense her own natural beauty was. She could look like The Grinch Who Stole Christmas, and she'd still be the most lovely woman he had ever set eyes on. Instead, he stubbed the toe of his wingtip Oxfords into the base of the chair two or three times. "It was my immense pleasure, Miss Rae."

She gave him the smallest of smiles, but it didn't reach her eyes. "Just Rae, Blaine. And thank you. Thank you so very much. This means more than you'd know."

He didn't want her to leave. Had he achieved the perfection she had been hoping for the last three visits? Would she be satisfied and never return? He reached out to help her up from the chair. She took his hand, her grip weak. Spontaneously, he joked, "You know that this style of perfection can only be achieved here at Upper Cuts by yours truly, right? So you have to return if you want to look like Maura all the time."

Was it the wrong thing to say? Her eyes fell. She shut her eyelids tight and took a deep breath. "Thank you. Yes, I've realized that. I'll be back, probably. I...I owe it to her. I owe her forever..." Her words trailed off.

Blaine's curiosity piqued, but he couldn't think of anything to ask quickly enough. He reluctantly released Rae's hand. She walked away from him toward the front, her flats padding almost silently across the tile. He followed her. "Ask for me again, please!" He bowed once more gallantly, hoping he looked silly enough to hide his infatuation with her.

She reached inside of her purse for her credit card and handed it to him. "I will." She smiled again.

Blaine glanced down at the card. "Rae Carrington," it said in gold capital letters across the card's face. He longed to take his time scanning the payment, holding her there in his shop, ogling her beautiful haircut and face for longer. But all too soon she was reaching for her raincoat, imprisoning his masterpiece underneath the thick hood, and shutting out his gaze by turning her back on him and exiting the salon. The bell jangled as she disappeared out the glass door, gone so quickly Blaine almost wondered for a second if she had existed at all.

That evening, back in his apartment four floors above the bustling city below him, Blaine stroked the smooth straight white fur of his Persian cat, Aphrodite. He welcomed the quiet, recharging in the solitude, the aroma of olive oil and rosemary, and the distant rumbles of city sounds that meant he was home. Hayley Westenra set up to play through the speakers, his hands found their memorized pattern on Aphrodite's back, and he welcomed the soothing calm of the cat's familiar feel under his palm. The vibrations of her purrs under his fingers massaged him after a long day. His shoulders and feet ached.

But his mind was still active – jumping rapidly back to Rae Carrington. Rae, made of soft pinks, vintage golds, sad blues and earthy browns. Rae who only wanted to look like Maura. Rae and her troupe of tears. Rae and her curls that felt like grandmother's quilts and summer nights. Rae who seemed from a different era and time. Rae and her new wispy bangs so delicate they were like fragile heartstrings breaking when he snipped them - every snip of his scissors coaxing out fresh tears. The intimacy of putting his hands through a stranger's hair, the personal touch that welcomed openness and emotions. The thought that he might see her again. The determination that he wanted to help her.

Blaine reluctantly released the cat and reached for his Bible. Time to catch some valuable reading to quiet his mind in order to sleep. Otherwise, he was preparing for a long night.

All week Blaine thought about her – how he wished he had gotten her phone number. But it was stupid to ask a lovely stranger for her phone number. How he wished he had used a cheesy line about destiny. But cheesy lines were stupid and she would've never come back.

He had Googled celebrities named Mara and Maura and Moira, and come up with no one who even came close to looking like Rae. He was stumped.

Then he laughed at himself for caring and being interested at all, threw himself into playful, friendly chatter with all of his other clients, and inwardly smacked himself whenever he thought of those sad doe eyes and glittery tears. He tried to just pray for her and move on, but she was this pinpoint of light in his recent history – things seemed to be defined by "Before His Masterpiece of Rae's Hair" and "After His Masterpiece." Cutting

James T. York's hair had been a life-changing moment – an occasion that earned him respect and reconciliation with his father. But cutting Rae's hair and receiving her tears and comment about "perfection" felt like he had accomplished his Mona Lisa. How could he improve upon last week if she returned? The thought of her coming back and wanting a new masterpiece gave him as much dread as it did hope in seeing her again. He stayed calm and lighthearted at work during the day, but every night he sat with Aphrodite next to him, his hands skittering over her back until she swiped at him to leave her alone.

All week he procrastinated on devising a plan for Rae's next haircut, should she return to the salon the following Wednesday evening. Every day he'd tell himself he needed to come up with another winning hairstyle for his new favorite client, and every day he grumbled, gave up, and went straight to bed with a mug of white tea and the Turner Classic Movies channel on low volume. He fell asleep to Gregory Peck or Audrey Hepburn, avoiding thoughts of Rae, trusting his instinctive, masterful hands to do their work when called upon in the eleventh hour. All he had to do was touch Rae's hair, and he'd create a new plan of perfection, he was sure. He hoped.

She entered right at five in the afternoon the very next Wednesday. Blaine had cleared his schedule just in case. He dropped the Better Homes and Gardens magazine he had been bored enough to flip through as he waited, and tried not to skid on the tile as he hurried to the counter to greet her. Biting his tongue, he forced himself to slow his jittery steps. He wanted to see her, but he had absolutely no idea how to wow her again with her hair.

"Rae!" was all he said, as she wrote her name on the clipboard.

94

She looked up, her eyes still hooded in sadness. Her mouth was a downward slope. "Blaine."

She remembered his name! The sound of it in the tones of her satiny sweet voice was like caramel to his brain. He realized he was grinning.

She removed her coat and hood, hanging it up. Her hair had gone flat, the curls disappeared, but she had kept up the wispy bangs. She fluffed them with her fingers, and they fluttered on her forehead like a greeting from a long-lost friend.

Blaine cleared his throat and waited, wringing his miracle-making hands in front of him — fingers longing to run themselves through her sadly lifeless tresses.

Rae glanced at him quickly, and then looked down at her heels. She wore black shoes and a matching black dress today. The color brought out the light tones in her brown sugar hair. "Can I just get a shampoo today and then... you can do what you did last week? Like with the curls and all? No trim. Just a styling?"

Blaine let out his breath in relief. "Yes, absolutely. I'd be delighted. Sounds good to me. You like what I did last week then?" He jabbered as he led her back to the sinks, his hand extended to guide her. He put his other hand gently on her back and then realized what he had done a second later. Too late. To pull his hand back now would make things awkward, so he simply pressed her forward.

She gave him the slightest of smiles. "Yeah, of course. It was just what I wanted."

Blaine warmed from his feet in his navy suede Puma shoes to the collar of his baby blue sport jacket. Tongue-tied, he waited for Rae to seat herself comfortably in the chair and lean her neck back onto the waiting terry cloth towel. He reached under her head and pulled all of her hair backward, smoothing out each strand.

Rae shut her eyes, her hands clutching her purse tightly.

"Want me to set that down for you?" Blaine offered. He reached for her purse strap and she relinquished it without opening her eyes. Setting it under her chair, he returned to stroking her hair, waiting for the water to warm. He watched her shoulders relax and sink deeper into the seat, her arms dropping to her sides.

He sprayed the soft jets over her hair, watching in a daze as the docile brown locks went heavy with water, darkening to a rich chocolate in his hands, falling as limp as her shoulders. Wracking his brain for something to say, Blaine could feel his chest tighten with each awkward passing moment.

And then, when he moved to hold the nape of her neck, he felt a drop hit the heel of his hand – a drop that could not have come from the sink. Lukewarm and lonely, a second simple pinprick of wet slid onto his hand and dissolved. It took him only a millisecond before he realized where they had come from. He searched Rae's face and saw a third tear forming at the far corner of her eye, fleeing to run straight past her ear.

Blaine's throat caught. She wasn't crying because she was fantasizing about how beautiful her hair would look when he was done. Something about merely getting her hair stylized was causing her much distress. Yet still she came back, resolved to spend money every Wednesday at Upper Cuts, trying to look like "Maura."

Not wanting Rae to be ashamed of her tears, and hoping to give her a moment of privacy to cry, Blaine found a hand towel underneath the sink, part of a stack in a back corner of the cabinet. Gently, he laid it across her face, covering her eyes and nose. Only her quivering bottom lip was exposed, and it shook sporadically. It hurt him to see it in the pit of his stomach. He wished he could calm and still that rosy lip with a kiss from his own mouth. And then he internally kicked himself for imagining kissing her at all.

Closing his own eyes, Blaine let the compassion that had sprung up like a sparkler in his heart flow down his veins into his arms, hands, and fingers. He massaged Rae's head in the most tender way he knew how. Like a parent soothing a sobbing child who had dreamed of the bogeyman, he caressed her head, massaging the shampoo into her scalp, and coaxing it back out again with the gentle jets of water.

When he had finished, after lengthening the time she spent under the water to twice as long as his other clients, he delicately wrapped her hair in a big fluffy white towel and pulled the hand cloth off her face. Her cheeks and temple were flushed but serene, and she stared him straight in the eyes without shyness or fear. Inquiringly, her gaze searched his.

Blaine's collar warmed once more, and he played with the rolled up sleeves of his sport jacket, breaking eye contact first. "Come on over to my chair and I'll blow dry your hair," he offered, biting his lip and looking away.

She stood up and stumbled, possibly feeling dizzy from her cry. She put a hand to the towel on her head, and reached out to grasp the sink to steady herself. Cursing himself for not having helped her up like a gentleman, Blaine reached out for her. Somehow, she ended up transferring her weight-bearing hand to his shoulder and leaned into him. He caught her around the waist, and she lowered her head to his chest.

Had he been transferred into a black and white oldie, like the ones that he watched on Saturday nights with a hot pizza and a fizzy Italian soda? He felt like

Frank Sinatra himself, the beauty in high heels hanging onto his arm.

Marguerite had to be staring. Her client was probably smirking. For once, Blaine didn't know and didn't care. His senses were turned off – all except his chest and arms that were cradling Rae.

She sighed and released him, stepping back and returning both hands to the towel on her head. "Thank you." She sighed and dropped her gaze. "I know you care. I could tell. Thank you for the privacy you gave me. Thanks for letting me come here to… grieve and… and tolerating me. I'm sorry I keep crying on you." She said her words in a halted whisper, as if rehearsing lines she had practiced on the way over.

Blaine fought the lump rising in his throat, the urge to shed tears with her. He motioned her to the chair silently, and she sat. Switching on the blow dryer, he stared into her eyes through the mirror while he tousled her wet locks in hot air. She didn't look away from him, but gave him brave eye contact, and Blaine felt like they understood each other without words. She didn't cry, and her mouth looked determined.

When her hair was dry, Blaine finally broke her powerful gaze, feeling as if his heart snapped at the same time. He took the brush and the curling iron and styled her hair in complete silence.

When she was complete, looking like she had the previous week, her gentle beauty shining below him, he finally stepped in front of her and sat on the edge of his counter. Perched with his legs and shoes stretched out in front of him, he leaned forward and met her eyes once more. "So who's Maura? An actress or something?"

Her chin trembled, confirming she meant someone far more personal.

Bravely, Blaine pushed forward. "Would you like to talk about her?"

She ran her fingers through her bangs and then dropped her hands to clasp them in her lap.

Blaine took a deep breath. "I would love to listen if you need someone to talk to." And then he was silent and waited.

Rae heaved a sigh and rubbed her temples. "She was my little sister." She glanced back at her reflection over his shoulder. "She was ten years younger than I am – only fourteen – and she looked like a younger version of how I do now. She was the sweetest little angel on earth."

Blaine's chest was suddenly smothered in a heavy weight. Past tense? "What happened?" he murmured.

Rae lifted eyes swimming in wetness to his. "She was…" She took a shaky breath. "She was hit by a drunk driver while crossing the street a few blocks from here. We were out shopping together. It was supposed to be together time – just the two of us – but I was caught up in work. I was on the phone with my boss – I'm way too busy most of the time – and I wasn't truly enjoying our time together. I was distracted and irritable, Maura was walking too slow, taking too long to window shop… I had errands to get to, and regretted dragging her along. I was the worst older sister, and Maura probably knew it.

"We passed by your salon that day, and Maura stopped to look inside. 'Mom always cuts our hair, but you should go get yours professionally done sometime, Rae,' she said. 'You're so beautiful – you could look like a celebrity.'" Rae waved her hand as if the lines embarrassed her to repeat. "She was such a vivacious and joyful little thing and she was suddenly like, 'Let's go get our hair done now! I'll pay you back. And I want to see how they can fix *you* up. You don't do anything nice with your hair!'

"I was impatient, and had no desire to go to a beauty salon. I yanked my hand out of hers and said a ton of stupid, hateful stuff about how she wastes time and is the slowest person I've ever seen…" Rae's voice crumbled. "So I just left and sped up down the sidewalk, not looking back. I got like two blocks ahead and didn't even care." Rae stopped and didn't speak for a long minute, her eyes shut in a tight line. "I had to cross the street, and she was trying to catch up. I could hear her running behind me. That's when the drunk driver ran the red light and hit her."

Tears had pooled in Blaine's eyes, matching the ones trailing down Rae's cheeks again. "I'm so sorry," he muttered, shaking his head.

In an intense but almost silent noise, soft enough that no one else in the salon could possibly hear it, Rae moaned, "If only I had stopped – made time in my day for a little haircut with my baby sister – we wouldn't have been anywhere *near* that intersection where the car was! If only I had realized my time with her was precious and just done something crazy and just gotten my hair done with her! I wish I had another chance!"

Blaine's breath came out noisily through his mouth. Rae's face was twisted, her hands clenched in her lap, her eyes full of wild agony. Her tears came furiously now, and she swiped at them.

"She died on a Wednesday a month ago, and, ever since, I've been coming to stare at the spot that she died, to bring her a red rose – her favorite flower – and lay it on the curb. Then I stop at the salon and pay my debt to her, getting my hair done every single week to pay back my guilt – to be the celebrity she wanted me to be. To live a little and do something she would have approved of. To slow down and stare in shop windows. To be the sister I should've been – the beautiful sister she thought I was instead of the ugly monster who rushed her along, only thinking about work when I should've been spending time with her!" Rae's voice rose in pitch, her sobbing intensifying. She threw the heel of her palms over her mouth and curled in on herself, great rivers of tears leaking underneath her hands. Her fingers clenched over her eyes as if trying to shut out her surroundings.

Horrified, Blaine reached for her, drawing her back into his arms, but by this time, everyone in the salon had stopped and was staring. Marguerite shot Blaine a wide-eyed look, her dye brushes forgotten in one hand.

Rae pushed Blaine away and ripped off the barber's cape. Running back for her purse, which had been forgotten next to the sink, she fumbled through her wallet, gasping for breath, tears still gushing from her eyes. Clutching a wad of cash, she shoved it into

Blaine's hand and ran from him, heels clicking, head down.

Blaine reached for her, but his hand fumbled with the bills, and he missed, grasping at air, tens floating down in dizzy waves at his feet. "Rae, wait!" he called, but her black dress disappeared through the front door with a jingle of bells, the jarring sound of it an affront to the depressing scene that had occurred.

The salon was completely silent save for the sounds of IZ's "Somewhere Over the Rainbow" mocking Blaine's already torn heart. He rubbed the bridge of his nose, smoothing away the lingering moisture, and ignored an open-mouthed Marguerite, praying she wouldn't say a word. Crouching, he gathered up the bills, his hands shaking. Then, with clipped steps, he made a beeline for the backroom to collapse into a hard plastic chair and simply ache.

An hour later, Blaine locked up the shop, sport jacket over one arm, his temples complaining. After the last customer had gone, Marguerite had come through the backroom, squeezed him on the shoulder, and asked a ton of questions. Blaine had given her the briefest of answers, hoping, with every word, that she would just disappear and not ask anything further. Finally, she had given him back his brooding silence, telling him the front door would be locked and the lights turned off. Telling him to take his time.

He found himself heading away from the salon the wrong direction from home. He realized he had no idea of where Maura had died, and he could cross the busy city streets all evening long without success. Still he continued, enveloping himself in darkening cool air to refresh his bruised heart and sore head. He kept his gaze at his feet, scanning curbs, looking for Rae's telltale rose.

Couples dressed to the nines clipped past him, men in Dockers and starched collared shirts with arms around women in slinky dark gowns. Bright lipstick and curls adorned most of the women, smiling and socializing, some perched pristinely in outdoor café chairs, sipping cocktails and enjoying their dates. But each woman blurred in front of Blaine's vision, none of them Rae, who had sparkled in melancholy beauty.

The sidewalks, dulled and grey, victims of decades of weather, shoe soles, and stroller wheels, looked exactly the same block after block. Blaine scanned every corner for a mile before turning around and heading back the way he came. Sighing wearily, his shoulders sagged and brow knit, new stabbing headache pains hitting his temples. Cigarette smoke wafted from a set of tables on his right, and he instinctively held his breath. His bones ached all the way down to the marrow.

There! A mere block past his salon in the right direction toward home – a blood red rose! Petals littering the asphalt below the curb, Blaine could tell it had been trodden on, and the sight brought sudden anger to his slumped back. He bent down to pick up the forlorn bits separated from the stalk, and laid them next to their mother flower. Then he sat down on the grimy curb, ignoring his light grey slacks, and stared at the rose. Blaine's throat seemed to shrink in on itself, his eyes becoming heavy with tears once again.

This was where Maura had died.

The rose lay, lonely and bright, striking him with its brazen bravery. Here in the loud chaos, exhaust fumes wafting over it frequently from head to toe, it kept sentry over the resting place of one woman's worst nightmare. Knowing it didn't belong on a New York City curb any more than a Louis Vuitton bag in a hobo's shopping cart, the rose shouted its existence anyway – all from the height of a large beetle.

Blaine's eyes darted back and forth and he found his hand reaching out in spite of himself. He plucked one of the fallen petals between two fingers and slipped it into his sport jacket's breast pocket. Then, feeling comforted, he blew a kiss to the courageous solitary blossom and picked himself wearily out of the street.

Rae didn't return.

Week after week, Blaine found his chest tightening when the clock hands finally made it to five on Wednesday afternoons. His eyes creeping to the door over and over again until he was almost dizzy, his heart died a little bit each week she didn't show.

After the third Wednesday without Rae, he found the nearest flower shop, three blocks down, and slipped out after salon hours to buy a single red rose. Full of nervous energy, he brought it to the street to lay it next to Rae's, and found the curb empty. She had not been by to drop her memento? He wiped sudden moisture from his eyes. Had telling her story scared her away forever? Would she never return to the salon or place a rose again on the street where Maura had died?

Each Wednesday after, Blaine hurried to the florist as soon as the door closed on his own salon. He always took his time scanning the bouquets, choosing the single fullest and heartiest blossom out of the bunch. He picked from those that were de-thorned, not wanting to stab a passerby if they happened to step on it. With dying hope, he strode to the same street corner, waited until he was sure no one was staring right at him, and kissed the rose, placing it softly down on the edge of the curb. It was always alone. Rae never again came by to share the space with a flower of her own, never to couple their roses together in solidarity to memorialize Maura together.

Each week he told himself it should be his last – that he should quit the practice altogether. That Rae had clearly moved on from needing to pay penance to her guilt. That telling her story to him must have freed her conscience and closed that chapter of her life.

But he didn't believe it. He vividly remembered those bills floating around him, her face streaked with tears, shame clinging to every inch of her body as she fled. Instead, by asking her to tell her story, he had scared her away from the one place she had been coming to grieve. He hated himself for that. He had severed any future healing for Rae like a snip from his scissors.

Bowed with a desperate worry of what had become of her, his mind drifted into numb hibernation with the coming winter. Buying his single rose became second nature. He did it without thinking, laying it often in banks of grey-stained snow, imagining he'd never stop. Imagining it was he who was paying penance now.

Half a year later, spring began to show its sweet head over the edge of the high rises around Upper Cuts. Dogwoods thriving in squares of dirt cut out of the sidewalks shyly slipped into full bloom overnight. Birds chased each other over the tops of preoccupied executives' heads. Young women of all ages arrived at the salon in droves, requesting new dos for everything from proms to weddings. Fresh shades of pink blazed in their cheeks, and bright Easter dresses were pulled sleepily out of musty closets.

He was trimming the straight wispy strands of an active six-year-old, her legs twitching, lollipop stuck in her cheek like a chipmunk, and his mind drifted. He contemplated going home for Easter, visiting his old church, and spending time getting intimate with his mother's famous pot roast. He could almost taste the homemade gravy and lemon meringue pie that would follow, his mother's natural talents coming out in full parade on the holiday. He was busy salivating, his scissors swishing under his hand, when the door chime rang.

"Welcome!" Marguerite's voice rang out in habitual cheerfulness. Then, "Blaine." Her voice cut into his meandering foody thoughts like a knife right through his imaginary pie.

He whipped his head up, his hands freezing in mid-air.

Rae.

What day was it? Was it Wednesday? Was it five o'clock? He almost didn't recognize her. She stood in the front door in babydoll pink, her soft, light sweater as fuzzy as a baby chick. Her hair had gotten long, and it hung to her upper arms in soft waves. She had kept the bangs though, and they stood at attention, as if saluting him like they were honoring their maker.

And then her eyes met his, and she smiled!

Blaine's heart pounding furiously, his vision swimming, he held up a finger to her, begging her to wait for him. He finished the child's hair in record time, rushing to the front counter to accept her mother's credit card and hurriedly send them on their way. Aware of Rae standing so close in the sitting area, he held his breath for great lengths of time until the child's mother signed the receipt and bid him goodbye.

Then Blaine stood behind the register and just looked at her. He was afraid to step out from the safety of the glass counter fencing him in like an overprotective matriarch. It was one o'clock on a Friday. What was she doing here?

Rae, the soft shy smile still lighting up her face, stepped forward towards him. He found himself giving a small gasp under his breath and scuffling backward a step. "Hi, Blaine," she said simply.

"Are you all right? What happened to you? Was it my fault for asking last time? Are you okay? I was worried about you..." The words came tumbling out of Blaine's mouth quietly, unbidden and rapid fire.

Rae sighed and rested her hands on the counter, her face a mere foot and a half from his. "I'm much better now." She took a deep, long breath and ran a hand through the bangs he had created for her, the ones she clearly kept trimmed so faithfully. "For a while I just couldn't come back... not after I had told you everything. It hurt too much. I don't know why I had been coming every week anyway. Getting my hair styled over and over again wasn't going to make Maura come back." Her voice shook. "I felt so guilty I wanted to die, and I hit a really low depression after I told you the story."

Blaine was drinking in every word she said but suddenly snapped to. What if someone else in the salon could hear? "Do you want to go outside for a minute?" he cut in. "I want to hear the whole thing, but want to give you some privacy." Bravely, he stepped outside of his glass fortress and gallantly offered her an arm.

She took it and smiled at him. "Thank you," she said, eyes glistening.

Blaine thought he might be falling in love with her, but that would be crazy, wouldn't it?

Outside, he searched frantically for a bench or any place to sit, but Rae tugged on his arm, leading him forward. They walked for a short ways and then came to

The Street – the place where Maura had been hit by the car.

There sat Blaine's rose. He always wondered how long the flowers lasted before they were stolen, tossed, or trampled to death. He knew they didn't make it a full week, as he never once saw one of his roses again, but now he had proof that they sometimes survived at least two days. There it perched limply, hugging the curb, its own petals floating around it like an injured animal. Horrified, Blaine released her arm and bent to gather the fallen red petals, shoving them into his pocket. He spun to find Rae sitting on the curb behind him, a look he couldn't identify on her face.

"I... I'm sorry." His cheeks were hot, and he wanted to disappear into the gutter.

"For what?" she asked softly, staring at him in a way that fanned the flames in his face to a dangerous level.

"For… for doing this…"

She reached for him. He sat and she took his hand. Her long fingers wrapped around his, her palm nestled against his. She covered the tips of his fingers with her second hand. Blaine's body melted to the pavement, every limb melted like butter. He couldn't move, his eyes fixed on Rae's face, his hand that she held singing with joy.

She looked out at the cars and taxis streaming by, and then back into his face. "For a while I couldn't come back to this spot. I couldn't come to your beauty salon or this street. I hated myself, and I wanted to die. Finally, after months of this, my parents begged me to go to grief counseling with them, and signed me up without telling me about it. They forced me to go. And, after a bunch of sessions, my counselor suggested I come visit the spot she died once again – she was afraid it had become like a trauma or fear of mine. She thought I needed closure –

not to leave roses, not to apologize any more. She said God had forgiven me and I needed to open my heart to Him and let His forgiveness wash me clean.

"So I came. And I saw a rose just lying there!" She waved a hand at the curb. "At first I thought maybe God had left it for me. I chalked it up to a really amazing miraculous coincidence. I felt healed that day. Peace washed over me. I'll never ever forget or stop missing my baby sister, but I felt like I could forgive myself and could start to be okay with the fact that I was still alive and she wasn't.

"But then, a few weeks later, I sat and really thought about that rose, wondering until I couldn't sleep. The next Wednesday, after I got off work, I walked down to this street, nervous, not knowing if I wanted it to be there or not. But there it was! Your rose."

Blaine bit his lip, looked at his feet, and tried to retrieve his hand. "I'm sorry..." he repeated.

Rae ignored him, grasping his hand tighter. "The next week I waited in that ice cream shop across the street. I showed up at five pm and waited two hours, sipping a coffee anc watching for you. And right at seven, there you were. You came to the curb, kissed the rose, and laid it down before walking past."

Blaine peeked up at Rae's face. Her eyes were shining.

"At first I was so touched I just sat at that window booth and cried. But the next two weeks – including last week – I just showed up and watched you. Always, right at seven pm, you brought the rose by. Have you been doing this for the last six months?"

Blaine nodded. His throat was too tight to speak. His blood pumped sporadically through his veins. He couldn't keep eye contact, but stared at their joined hands in growing terror.

Rae leaned down and kissed the back of his hand, dousing all of his fears in an instant. His mouth dropped open and closed again, and he swallowed rapidly. He looked up at her in shock. The bright blazing sunshine overhead hugged her in golden light, framing her milk chocolate tresses like a halo. It bounced off of her form to strike the whole world around them, brightening the colors to full saturation.

"Thank you, dear Blaine," she said. "I don't even know you, but you must have the sweetest heart of any man in Manhattan. To remember me and remember my sister... and keep bringing a rose each Wednesday, even after I ran out on you..." She hesitated and then plowed forward, her words coming faster. "I want to get to know you, Blaine, if that's okay. Like I want to bring you home and meet my family! Heck, I even want to take you to Maura's grave!" Tears sparked in her eyes once more. "You have shown my sister more honor and devotion than any of our closest friends."

Blaine began to protest, but Rae dropped his hand and stood up. "I got the rest of today off. I looked it up and know your salon closes early on Fridays. Can I take you out? I'd like to treat you to an early dinner and a huge dessert and thank you. And maybe we can just talk. Will that be okay?"

Blaine stood on shaky feet and found his voice. Over the rush of traffic and the occasional chirp of a horn, with Rae's big doe eyes staring at him hopefully, he laughed. "More than okay!" He reached for her hand again. "Rae Carrington…" His mind took a snapshot of this moment. "This might just be the best day of my life."

Dedicated to the "forgotten counselors" – the beauticians, dental hygienists, masseuses, and moms on the playground... you do more than you know.

Aine, Starwarrior

With a silent scream exploding inside of her chest, Aine willed the intense pain to flee down her arm. Each second, the suffering lessened, and Aine knew that she need only to fling the glittering sky jewel, and it would be over.

As the wave of familiar torment washed over her, Aine held the star in her hand. It burned and fizzled, sparkling glitter light against her palm. The shock waves of pain subsided over her glistening fingers. The bright, hot, deathly beauty of it would always entrance her.

She flung it. Threw it from her with the might of a thousand starwarriors before her. The hot ball of gas spun and sputtered, flying end over end. It whirled toward the densely ebony being only a few light years from her, its ugly hide filling the entire span of a galaxy.

Aine herself stretched as tall as almost two thirds of the more popular Milky Way, not having come into her full height. Having lived only tens of thousands of years, she was a baby among her people, but one of the most talented starwarriors in millennia. Her raw talent kept her in high demand for the more difficult of battles – like the one she faced today.

The pain of catching the stars she used as weapons didn't deter her like it did some of her peers. She was accustomed to the sharp burning lightning bolts that ached through her entire body when she plucked the little gems out of the sky.

Monsters, like the one in front of her, swallowed up whole planetary systems, eliminating entire species of sentient beings. Bound to protect the universe, she galloped across the silent coldness of space she called home. She was transparent and crystal in color, her presence soothing and open. She was as quiet as the wind. The only time her heroic efforts went noticed was when beings pointed out shooting stars to each other. They made wishes on them. If only they knew that their very lives had once hung in the balance as Aine fought, flinging those balls of luminous gas. Their wishes drifted up to her thoughts, centuries later, fueling her, giving her purpose for new battles to come.

The failed starwarriors were the ones that dropped asteroids, allowing them to crash down on the planets they had sworn to protect. They were discharged, never to serve in battle again, but left to roam the galaxy in shame. Aine purposed to fight her best, to protect many, and to succeed with honor.

The monster swatted at the star, its opaque, hard skin rippling. In the silence of space, it made no sound, but opened its mouth to show it hurt from defending itself. Its mouth had many names, "black hole" being the one the humans used. Its hunger was never abated, and thriving planets were its favorite meal. It ate the star without a second thought, the burning subsiding in its throat, annihilated forever. A trail of iridescent dust was all that remained of the once glistening mass that Aine had thrown.

Closing her eyes and embracing the scorching torture with a finality bred of awareness of destiny and the vital importance of her mission, Aine hurdled handfuls of stars. This particular black hole creature was a major contender, not some small fry prey. He wouldn't give up easily.

The meteor shower of weapons was breathtaking, even to a starwarrior accustomed to the show. The sprinkling sparked awe in Aine's chest to join the agony her hands and arms threw down her waving, enormous limbs.

The black hole's mouth yawned. With gulps, it vanquished the first hoard of stars, shaking and glistening in rage, its hide knocking into other suns, bursting them to die against its flesh.

Aine leaped in a circle around it as it twisted and whirled, the dark fiend trying its best to obliterate the onslaught. Faster and faster Aine jumped, reaching careful hands to neighboring planets for balance as she pivoted, shaking their surfaces only as delicately as possible. She spun planets in orbit, and threw stars like knives.

At the height of her mental concentration, her limbs finally went numb. The burn marks turned into delicate trails of dust on her hands, scarring her. Still she continued, circling and leaping and throwing balls of gaseous fire.

The stars crashed into the monster and struck, one after another, as his mouth missed more and more, swallowing dead space instead, pulling planets out of their orbit around their suns. It started to bend against itself. As it raged, ever silently, against the stars burning its surface, its mouth turned inward. Slowly, it began to swallow itself, bit after bit, destroying itself to stop the torment.

Aine flashed with a sudden sympathetic ache for her enemy, as horrifically destructive as it was, imagining the scorching of tens of stars against her own translucent body. As the monster swallowed itself, the flashing hard outline of its hide began to disappear until, turning itself completely inside out, it swallowed the last of its mouth, obliterating itself out of existence.

Success.

Aine fell still, dropping the last star that sat searing her palm, leaving it to hang like a beacon of her victory where the gaping black hole had winked out. The trophy star drew planets toward itself slowly, but surely, their migratory path changing and healing itself. Worlds were saved this day.

Moving away slowly, she envisioned the lightyears of travel ahead of her. The exhausting battle was over. All she wanted to do was lie down in the void of space she called home. She would sleep for centuries, and awaken to fight again. This was her destiny. This was her purpose. Lives would be saved. She could feel the wishes that would return to her when the star show reached them down on their planets. Her joy complete, she continued her steady dance, as graceful as a deer, out through the galaxies to the outer regions of the universe.

Lucent Sylph

Lucent Sylphs.

The otherworldly pet for the 24th century American.

Own a translucent glass fairy that can sit in the palm of your hand. Own one of these fragile little beings – and you set yourself apart from everyone else.

I shuddered when I saw my former friend Josiah showing off his new Lucent Sylph at school at the beginning of the quarter. She sat there, crystal clear, pulsing heart and veins clearly visible beneath her see-through hard skin. Wings as solid as a thin sheet of glass, she eyed the ogling classmates with something like forced apathy, but I suspected she was nervous as well.

"Put her away." I murmured for Josiah's ear alone. "You, of all people, can't handle a Lucent Sylph."

Josiah ignored me. "Want to hear her name?" he asked the crowd.

"You named her?" I exclaimed. She was doomed.

Josiah motioned to me. "Lucas, my man! Sounds like you want to know. It's Nissa!"

Nissa.

I swallowed hard.

She looked at me. She turned her tiny, thumb-sized head and gazed at me, her eyes fathomless and deep. She could tell I feared for her. Emotions were not safe around these creatures.

Josiah had no self-control. She would die.

Lucent Sylphs sell themselves into slavery. It almost always means their death. It's just a matter of time.

Just under a million Lucent Sylphs pop through our atmosphere every year. They began their search to find our dimension when their failed economy meant certain death for a large portion of their population. They succeeded in reaching us two years ago, and their open hands and bowed necks, as well as their unique and delicate beauty, won them instant favor with the populace. The Lucent Sylphs' land of Sylpha is nearby in terms of coordinates on a map, but unreachable in all ways – a completely different dimension. The portal is located in The Field of Sylphs, four or five hours outside of Denver, where I live. They arrive as infants, burrowing into the ground to mature, instinctively following what was whispered to them by their mothers. They are sent here to provide for their kin, and help them survive.

They shoot through the portal, escaping famine, starvation, and desperation. Auctioning themselves off to eager buyers here in the United States, they send our cash, which is then traded into gold dust, back through the portal. A year later, the gold dust arrives in Sylpha by means of little beetle-sized pods they arrive with – a specific name printed on the sides – and are received by the family they were intended for. The gold is coveted in the land of Sylpha, and used to save their homes and relatives.

A Lucent Sylph does not eat or sleep, but is fueled on human emotion. Her insides consist of single giant heart and circulatory system that captures and feeds off of the strong feelings around her. Too much neglect or unkindness, and a Lucent Sylph will cloud over and disintegrate. Too much love and attachment, and the heart will be overcome and burst.

In an age where video games and virtual reality can take you anywhere in the universe you want to go, and let you experience whatever you want to be, my generation of teenage males are bored. Relationships have become exciting again, after so many holograms and so much fiction. But nothing old-fashioned is regarded as exciting. Relationships with humans are boring. Therefore, the newest thrill? Playing dangerous emotion games with a Lucent Sylph.

I know so few girls anymore who own one. Girls' hearts are easily touched, and the Lucent Sylphs tend to burst too easily, raining sparkles and shimmering powder all over the spot they last stood. I saw it in an online video once, and I'll admit that I cringed and my eyes grew damp. It isn't entertaining to watch someone kill a pet, especially one as intelligent and lovely as a Lucent Sylph.

But guys like me tend to succeed for a time. The fairies excite young males, interact with them, and make them feel like masculine protectors. Males tend to guard their hearts better, messing around, instead, with online RPG characters, created to have perfect curves and scripted lines. Fake projections who feel safe and easy.

Call me soft, but I did not relish taking a life into my own hands. Playing a dangerous juggling act with my heart, which was already so hard to understand, sounded like torture to me. To know I had extinguished life by my shifting, male, teenage hormones? No thank you.

Guys like Josiah lived on brutality games that made my stomach turn over. I preferred to read and draw. By middle school, we knew we were incompatible as friends.

Two weeks later and I had all but forgotten about Josiah's Nissa. It had been a long time since we had hung out.

I was walking past his neighborhood to get to the food disposal warehouse. My gaze swept the neighborhood aimlessly. The street was a typical one – full of high rise apartments crammed into tiny spaces. But then I noticed something sparkle in the gutter.

Stepping forward, I saw her. Her glassy body was cloudy, and her eyes misted over. It was Nissa, abandoned. She appeared to be committed to staying in the spot where her master had dumped her.

"Nissa!" I had vowed to never say a Lucent Sylph's name. Naming them meant attachment for humans. I didn't want to be on friendly terms with any of them. Killing someone else's Lucent Sylph would be like tearing up piles of cash.

"Can you stand? Can you fly?" I asked her, worriedly. She couldn't have been abandoned for long. The cloudiness had not overcome her heart yet.

"I can, but I must not. Master Josiah will return."

I had seen it coming. She must've shown signs of clouding, due to his irresponsibility and unkindness, and he had thrown her away, afraid to have her life in his hands after all. I balled my own hands into fists. "He won't, Nissa. You scare him and he's left you."

The mist filled in her glass head. I had sped up the process!

Reaching down, I scooped her gently up into my hands. She was lighter than I expected – no more than a cup of water. I covered her, closing my fingers over her, as if to shield her from the negative emotions seeping down like a stench from his apartment nearby. "Please don't die. I'm sorry. Josiah is a cretin and doesn't deserve you." I couldn't watch. I turned my head.

When nothing happened, I looked back down into my hands, opening my fingers a little.

Nissa sat, staring up at me, those luminous black eyes full of curiosity. The cloudiness was gone! I could see all of her veins, thin but transparent, pulsing faintly. Her heart beat steadily, and her eyes were clear.

Letting my breath out in a whoosh, I tried to place her down on the curb. She flew back up beside me, wings vibrating quicker than my vision could perceive.

"Master Josiah has thrown me away. I am free to attach myself to a new master."

"No!" I stumbled as I stepped backward quickly. "You are free. Go your way! Why can't you Lucent Sylphs simply make your home in our dimension and dwell peacefully with us? Why indenture yourselves to us and lose your lives? Take your freedom and go home."

"We must attach ourselves to someone who feels affection for us," she said simply, never losing eye contact with me. "There is no way to go back to Sylpha. I cannot."

This was news to me, but explained the question that had always bothered me. "Why not? Your pods return with the gold."

"The journey takes nearly one of your human years. As infants, we are held in a comatose state, nourished by the Love that birthed us. As adults, we cannot survive a journey more than a day without a source of emotion."

This was the reason the rest of the world could not get their hands on the Lucent Sylphs without traveling to our country and picking them up in person. You could not package up a Lucent Sylph in a box and send her, expecting her to make even an overnight trip without disintegrating. We were the envy of the world these days, our Sylphs bolstering our economy and making us a world power once more. Hordes were knocking at our borders, applying for travel visas, and looking for an excuse to enter.

"When we are first born out of a moment of deep adoration, our mother sends us away in our infant state, choosing, at birth, that we will be the saviors of our families. We chrysalize like your butterflies, and, in just over a year, we mature into the adults you see now. Your atmosphere hits our full-grown hearts, and we feel that we are starving. This sent us to find you human to keep us alive. Those that are not sold quickly despair and die."

"I don't know how to control my heart. You can't stay with me!" I insisted, putting my hand up to block her from my sight.

"Then sell me again. I will be yours until you find a buyer. I am sure you would like the money."

The thought of placing her in the hands of someone like Josiah pained me even more.

With the sound of fluttering that was barely audible, Nissa rose and did a graceful swan dive in the air. "You already care for me," she observed.

Cursing, I bowed my head. "I don't want to do this."

She swooped in close and landed delicate feet on my shoulder. "If you do not, you will feel regret, and your sadness will overwhelm me."

I looked up and, indeed, my troubled mind had caused some murkiness in her feet. Focusing on positive feelings toward her, I sent my thoughts forward, and the clouds in her feet dissioated as I watched.

"Until I find a buyer," I mumbled, and covered her with my hand.

Holding her between my palms, I felt the heat of her happy heart, mine drumming its own rapid and excited rhythm. I love too much. I am pathetic and weak. I am a teenage guy! I cannot do this!

Nissa attempted to lie on my pillow the first night, her body heating my closed eyelids.

"I will make you your own bed," I sighed. "You're too close and I might crush you."

Her happy nod grew her heart with another strong pulse, and I feared for her life.

"Plus, you're too warm, and I don't want you to annoy me," I added with a growl. It was a lie, and, like I feared, it did nothing to shrink her heart. My words were meaningless if my emotions did not follow suit. There was no deceiving a Lucent Sylph.

When she lay still, awake but obediently unmoving, in the shoebox full of my mother's softest shirt I had saved, I searched the Internet for information. Everyone had a different story. No one's Lucent Sylph died for a similar reason. There was no way to predict how much love was too much or when they would feel emotionally neglected.

That's the thrill of it! one former owner posted.

When was your first LS fail? queried one user.

How many have disintegrated on you?

Dude, how do you have that much $$$?

Little bugger died the next day I brought her home. Biggest waste of money ever.

It made me sick. I logged out of my computer portal and tried to sleep.

In the morning, I had a plan.

"You're going to go home," I said.

The Lucent Sylph were curious creatures, but emoted little. Nissa just gave me her wise stare. "No one has returned, Master Lucas. It is Loveless and impossible."

"Don't call me 'Master,'" I said, frustrated. "You are a free creature with a will of your own. I don't believe in slavery. I didn't buy you, remember? You came here of your own free will."

Her veins throbbed. I stared. They were as thin as the lines from my stylus that marked white across my handheld computer. I had drawn a Lucent Sylph once, the one in the online video, just to get her image out of my head. She had been sitting on her master's shoulder, and then something pushed her over the edge. The man recording the video had been trying to catch his son's virtual sports match, and caught the Sylph exploding instead.

Why had I viewed the video back then? I couldn't sleep or eat that night, unable to get it out of my head. Drawing the little delicate creature somehow freed it from my mind.

Looking at Nissa now, I realized there were many things about her kind that were not apparent in the video. Her heart was hot, but not too bright. Like a pulsing ball of fire that dimmed when the lights went out. Her veins were deep crimson, but tinted blue at the edges. Her face was featureless glass – no nose, and only a parting mouth that spoke. But her eyes were balls of ink, depth behind them. I felt as if I could find the age-old questions of the universe if I looked long enough.

But I was afraid to gaze – afraid that a bond would be formed which would doom the sensitive creature to an early death.

"Lucas," she called, the moment I awoke one day.

"Still enjoying the shoebox bed?"

"As soft as the Field of Sylph where I came into my own," she replied, and I took it to be the greatest compliment she could give.

"The shirt is silk. It was my mother's."

"You speak of her in past tense," Nissa said simply, her voice always soft, delicate, and unemotional.

"She died." It had been ten years. Taking a breath, and stuffing my messenger bag with my assigned text-handhelds for school, I didn't look at her. "I was six years old. It was a long sickness. I stayed by her hospital bed many nights."

She was quiet.

I found myself talking about something I always refused to discuss. That scared me. "It's just my father and me now. My father works late as a robotic bodyguard repairman. He comes home and watches the virtual television many hours into the night. He drinks. He's angry a lot. We avoid each other as much as possible."

"And you are gentle like your mother." She was astute.

I shrugged, embarrassed. "Tell me about your world over breakfast." I hurried to grab a piece of toast.

Slathering it with jam, I watched her hover in the air. "You had a mother too. Are you all female?"

She cocked her head. "We do not have a sex, but all look, more or less, as you see me. Your kind tends to associate us with your female gender."

"But not every Lucent Sylph looks exactly alike. One can tell his own apart from another," I argued, taking a bite of the sticky jam bread.

"We are not all the same."

"You are asexual," I mused. "You are born from one Lucent Sylph? Two aren't needed to come together?"

"I do not know what you mean," she replied. "But yes, we are born of one alone. Love is the atmosphere in Sylpha. Love created the land. We have no oxygen, no gravity, no plants, and no food. We have our homes and our skies full of color. We have communication and learning. We have endless stories. We live two hundred of your years."

"Then why the poverty? Why come find us and our gold and sell yourself?" I scrubbed my hands with a damp rag to remove the last traces of jam.

"We are crowded. Our 'sun,' or center of Love, extends only so far. When the reaches of Love end, we turn to dust and blow away. Homes within the boundary cost all one has. Many live under the elements, in cold and heat. We have no body over there, but are much more substantial in our emotional form."

"Why the delicate balance? Why aren't we allowed to care more about you here on earth? Or why can't we box you away and protect you? And how is an atmosphere made up of love? I can't comprehend it." I lingered, not wanting to leave her, my bag thumping against my bouncing leg. I wanted to ask every question I had ever pondered in the hours I could not sleep, listening to the wail of the virtual television below me, knowing my father wished I had died instead of my mother. Knowing he could not love me. Feeling alone and wondering how a Lucent Sylph must feel, having been sent away – only to die.

"You must think of it as oxygen. Too little and you humans suffocate. Too much and you cannot bear its weight. The balance must be precise. It is the same for us. We do not feed off of each other, as our own feelings cannot transfer into sustenance. But, in Sylph, the center, or sun of Love, exists brightly and keeps things at a natural balance. When we die there naturally, we are sucked back into it, and turned into life-giving Love to sustain others. It is, truly, a circle of life.

"For so long, we were too Lovefull. Many Lucent Sylphs were born, and too few died. There was not enough Love to extend the boundaries. Our over-population created despair, as Sylphs were forced out into the farthest reaches where they starved and died. Sending great quantities of us to your dimension gives us something to barter with – gold – and keeps our numbers at a reasonable rate."

"That's so unfair for you!" I cried.

She glowed a little, but said nothing.

"If I go to school now, and leave you in my room, will you be here when I get back?" My voice shook, in spite of itself. I was so very afraid.

"Your worry for me has given me strength," she replied, and her veins dilated in response to my aching chest.

Shutting off my feelings, as firmly as I could, I turned away from her. "Have you ever used a holographic telephone? There's one on the desk, with my caller ID. If you press it, you can reach me. I will be able to see you and assess damage."

"Josiah abandoned me and I did not die." There was no bitterness in her voice, only fact. "You should not worry about a day of classes."

"Do not come out of my room. My dad sometimes stops by for lunch. Don't let him see you. Not only will he mock me, but he despises fragile things." I dropped my voice to a whisper. "Because of my mother."

I chose to look back, against my better judgment, and we made eye contact. "Goodbye, Nissa," I murmured.

"Goodbye, Lucas." Her chest burned bright.

"Not even staying to play, Thissel?"

We stood in the rec room at the back of the school. The shiny white virtual reality portals glistened with sweat, smoke, and flashing lights.

"Lucas! You have to beat Josiah!" Meagan whined. "He keeps saying he's slain more dragons than our entire class!"

Josiah had all of the girls. They flocked to him for his gaming power. His virtual muscles enticed them.

"He wouldn't even be worth my time," I called back. I was in a hurry to get home. Nissa had not called, but I wasn't even sure she would if she needed to. The Lucent Sylphs didn't seem to have a very strong sense of self-preservation.

"Lucas Thissel," Josiah roared, lifting his opaque goggles off of his red-rimmed eyes. He lifted his gloved finger, yanking the wires along with him as he pointed at me. "Resident girly man." He turned to Megan and the other girls. "He's been too chicken to play me for some time."

"You wish, show-off. I'm not wasting time beating you to a pulp." I raised a hand and sent a frigid smile their way. Sure, let me be chicken. Just let me go.

Meagan looked disappointed. She was eyeing me.

I blinked. She was head popular girl, and the owner of the nicest set of portal computers. Her homemade player skins were the talk of our school.

Flushed and confused, I didn't give her a second glance. Better not to show any interest in return. What she didn't know was that I was weakling boy who liked old-fashioned paintings and had an abusive father. Not much point in bringing a girl home.

Especially an emotionally-charged glass girl.

Yet there she was back in my room. Cloudiness had set in at the tips of her fingers, which made me want to choke on my own throat, but she reassured me that it was normal. My return made the mist in her crystal clear body dissipate and vanish.

I breathed a sigh of relief, but my chest still felt tight. I would never be able to relax again. This was why I had not wanted a Lucent Sylph.

This was why I had rejected all *companionship.*

Had the loss of my mother broken me? Was I afraid of my own heart and how easily it shattered? Is that why I avoided everyone, preferring solitude and safety?

Bitterly sad, I lowered my head to my hands and sat on the edge of the bed.

Nissa sank to my shoulder and put her warm, delicate hand against my neck. Her fingers were hard and lighter than a drop of water, and yet they felt like a soft, heavy burden to me.

"I am sorry to cause you pain," she said. "We need your gold to survive, and we are honorable, giving our companionship in return for your emotion. However, we do not consider the suffering we put our human masters through. I have begun to realize what sorrow I cause you, and I want to set it right. I fault not Josiah Mullins. He was in pain."

"Josiah?" I laughed, a bit of scorn in my middle. "He cares for nothing but destruction. He can't love even if he tried."

"You are wrong," Nissa said quietly. Her glass hand stroked my neck. "He has much emotion in him. No one can hide this from one of us. He is merely a coward."

"*I'm* the coward," I burst, the new revelation of my hermitic habits still stabbing my chest.

"You are braver than he," she said. "Look at what you have done."

I slept close to her that night – I on my side, and she lay curled up on my cheek, eyelash to eyelash. Her steady warmth, which had grown quite hot, felt like the soothing weight of a tender hand. I did not know how I would live without her understanding and friendship.

And that thought kept my heart racing, even as I slept.

"How do you propose this plan will succeed?" Nissa asked, as she flitted around me.

We were out at Meadow's Park overlooking the city. One of the few areas not covered with skyscrapers, the hill felt like heaven to me. "You think this is what people were trying to do with the Tower of Babel?" I asked, ignoring her question. "Get above the earth and feel safe and close to God?"

She stopped flitting to stroke a single blade of grass. Nuzzling it against her face, she seemed lost in thought.

"Do you know about God?" I asked her suddenly, crouching low to see what grass looked like through the lens of her body.

"We are made of Love," she said. "God is Love."

I smiled. "Indeed He is." I had never doubted that fact, even when Mother was taken from me. It was *I* who had a hard time accepting the dangerous emotion.

She danced delicately, her wings a blur, her long legs and narrow feet skimming the surface of the ground. She threw her head back and twirled.

"This is what I love best about your dimension." She paused, and I thought she meant the sun. "Plants," was the final reply.

"Not our sun or our sky?"

She shook her head at me, her black eyes holding more mirth than I had ever seen in them. "We see your sun, but we feel not its warmth. It sits there, and does nothing for our souls. I do not enjoy the sun for its warmth, heat, or physical properties, but I can appreciate it for what it evokes in you. We are warmed by something you cannot see, Lucas. By something those in your dimension cannot prove. By something that just *is*, although no one can measure it. In my dimension, it takes form. And you see me here before you now."

"Is that why I can see through you? Is that why you are so small? Is that why you seem like a reflection in a mirror, and I can hardly believe that you are alive?"

She did not answer, but continued her dance, captivating me. I should take her outside more often.

Red filled her body, and her heart seemed to flame up. She came to a halt in the grass and looked up at me imploringly. "Think about the death of your mother if you would like me to live. Think about giving me away. Think about your father. I will not dance for you again."

162

And, as I focused on painful things long enough to bring tears to my eyes, her heart subsided back to its normal glow. A few of my tears were not for my mother or father, but because she said she would never dance for me again.

"Every day I will let you come out here and dance alone, if you please," I vowed. "I will stay at home, and you can return when you like."

"If I choose to do so, and come out from under your protection, I will let no other human capture me," she promised, and she seemed to sparkle with merriment again.

I felt the throb through my heart at her words, and I was powerless to stop it. "Back to my plan." I sought for a distraction. "Nissa, you should be able to go home."

"How?"

"They make miniscule microphones and chips and speakers. You would think some company has already thought of this and are working on one now. One with an extended battery!"

"What would be done with it?" she asked, confused.

"I could supply you with a tiny recorder that plays my words of love to you over and over again as you travel!"

Nissa's eyes flashed, for an instant, and she seemed to wince in pain. Flying up to lay her hands and cheek to my nose, she shook her tiny head at me. "Let us go home and talk no more of this for now, Lucas. I cannot bear your Love today."

Head drooping, I submitted, pushing her body away to fly on its own, putting distance between us.

"And Lucas," she added, her voice drifting behind me. "If you miss, even by one day, and the tiny chip dies? It would be better to stay by a master's side and be worth the gold that was paid for me."

"Micronano chips," they were called. And they functioned on an enhanced battery. One could buy them for a small fortune. Originally, they had been used by government agents, embedded in the ear canal for secret communication. Now they were offered to a small few who could go nowhere without constant music playing privately in their ear. The battery boasted a survival time of almost eighteen months. And I had a savings account.

"I will say the sweetest things I can think of. Things I have never said to anyone before," I murmured under my breath, self-conscious at the thought.

Pointing at my computer portal, I held Nissa up on two fingers to see the screen.

"What will you use to return me? I cannot fit into the pods we use to send back the dust."

"What are they made of?" I questioned eagerly. My fingers flew over the air in front of my screen, connecting with keys only my special goggles could see.

Sure enough, someone had dissected a pod, devastating the Lucent Sylph who arrived with it. Without a means for sending back gold, her life had been wasted, and she had disintegrated instantly, her distress so cruel that I could only shudder.

"Her death will not be in vain!" I declared.

The pod was made up of a simple element that most resembled iron. "Easy," I said. "Find an iron casing big enough for you and the chip."

Nissa's tiny hand stroked the tip of my finger. She had become very affectionate these days, every brush of her body against mine like a thrill running through both of us. I loved her more with each tender touch, and her heart responded to the emotion I extended. How long had it been since anyone touched me anyway? I wanted to protect her, like my own body, forever.

But I had to give her up. And soon. I could tell, in the sustained enlargement of her veins, that I was teetering on the brink.

She was my closest friend. We went to the hill often, although she never took me up on the offer to dance alone. She seemed loathe to leave my sight each day for school, and often waited for my return with a sandwich or some other concoction that she had labored over while I was gone. She once told me she had dragged a large chunk of salami all over the kitchen before getting her bearings and dropping it onto the waiting bread she had wrestled out of the bag.

Sometimes the foods she put together were inedible, and I laughed at her attempts, eating them anyway, my tongue content to play dumb. How long had it been since anyone cooked for me?

Other times I was awed by her feats.

"Spaghetti? How did you cook the noodles? I give you books to read on my handheld to pass the time, so why attempt this instead?"

"I have read them all," she complained. "Your father left water in a pot. I was able to push the buttons for the stove. Although, I fell into the pot once trying to stir."

"You fell into boiling water?" I was shocked.

She tittered at me, a laugh sound that I had never heard before from her, even after searching the Internet for the vocal patterns of a Sylph. "I was not burned. I have no skin to burn. I am unharmed by the tangible dangers of your world. It is the intangible things that are lethal."

Always the reminder of our limited time.

"I bought a cast iron canister big enough to hold you. Air tight!" I cheered one afternoon.

She swayed to the music I played in my room. "This is beautiful," she said. Like the outdoors, I had come to realize that art, of all kinds, reminded her a little of home. "It is the closest you humans get to proving and measuring Love," she once explained, cryptically.

Now she turned to me, watching my face. "Iron canister? Air tight matters not. I do not breathe."

"But what is the atmosphere like traveling through the portal? Could it harm you?"

"No." And she was back to swaying, seated on my desk, her hand resting on mine.

"I wonder if I could hold it," I mused playfully. I turned my palm over and tried to grasp hers, but it was almost lost deep inside of mine.

"I will do this instead," she offered, and lay face down across my palm, extending to grasp all of my fingers in a full-body hug. She looked up at me, almost coy – pleased with herself. I was reading her subtle personality better these days.

I love you, I wanted to say. It was on the tip of my tongue. I even opened my mouth.

"I know," she replied, as if I had spoken. "I Love you too."

Struggling to keep my heart cool, I confronted her. "Isn't that a death wish? Can you love too?"

"It does me no harm to Love you. I cannot feed or harm myself with my own thoughts. It is only yours that nurture me. So I am free to Love you with the full breadth of my heart."

I looked at her and flushed miserably, my eyes boring holes into hers.

She doubled over, her body full of blood red color.

Panicking, I flung her from me.

She went careening about my room, her wings as rapid as bullets.

I let myself out of the house and ran to the hill of Meadow Park. I was a coward for leaving her to suffer. I was a coward for not letting her go sooner.

If she was still alive when I returned, she needed to go.

We took the bus, Nissa hidden in my shirt pocket, warming a spot against my chest. It was a long day's ride. Overcome with what we were doing, I said very little.

When we arrived, I was aghast at what we found.

"I warned you of this. The Field of Sylphs is heavily guarded by your military. How are you going to get through?" Nissa asked the question I did not want to answer.

"People show up wanting to donate gold dust all the time and trying to get close to the portal," I reassured myself. "No one ever lets them do it, though, because of the stupid buyer-seller market we've created. Americans are greedy, and you give us what we want."

She raised her head and pointed her eyes upward. "Your charity would not have been honestly earned. Nor would it arrive in a pre-marked pod. It would be rejected. We have our honor." Nissa seemed to grow four inches after her grand speech. She held her chest high.

"Does the gold keep its physical state over in Sylpha?"

She stared at me, patient with my questions. "Nothing has a 'physical state' in Sylpha. But the emotional property of gold is the closest to our life-giving Love. It is a copycat, but it suffices."

The fascinating thing was that a scientist had assessed the exploded sparkly dust of an emotionally overwhelmed Lucent Sylph, and the elemental components were indeed closest to gold in raw form.

"So gold is love, eh?" I smirked. "I know a lot of greedy Americans who would agree."

At the highly protected border of the acre-long Field of Sylphs, my heart quailed. "How can a skinny guy get past that armamert?" I murmured.

Nissa sat perched on my head. She wrapped strands of my hair around her arms, gently tugging. "Dear Lucas. You were admirable to attempt it."

"Don't give up row!" I reached up and popped her lightly on the head.

She caught my hand and held it to her middle, like a shield and a comfort.

I wrapped my fingers around her hard core. We had to try. I sighed shakily. "Let's wait for more tourists. I hear there's a tour at noon."

We entered with five different languages, a swirl of incomprehensible words proceeding from the mouths of our giant group of visitors.

"How did you learn English?" I whispered to my shirt pocket where she was hiding. I realized I had never asked the most obvious question of all. Dropping my chin to hear her words, her reply came up faintly.

"Language is but an expression of your feelings and soul. We read it in its most emotional form. It is not hard for us to speak whatever we wish. It is intangible and unmeasured, therefore it is of us."

I nodded, satisfied for now.

The heavy canister was a weight in my largest messenger bag. It dug against my shoulder, a reminder of the deep pain that would be mine that day. I shook my head, choosing to pretend it did not exist. I protected Nissa that way, as well as myself.

As we came to a viewing platform, I saw a steel ladder that extended down to the field. Guard towers and cameras covered every inch of the border. In the center, hovering above the tall spikes of grass, a shimmery spot of sky bucked and waved across the landscape.

"On some days, you can see a pod arrive through the portal, or even a Lucent Sylph rise from the ground where she spent her time completing her maturation," explained the tour gu de, a small brunette with a gentle voice. She seemed happy doing her job. "We sell them right here in our official store, and are one of the few legal sources for these precious pets. Of course, you need to be eighteen years or older to buy one. They are sold cheaply on the black market, but are usually already clouded over from mistreatment. Many do not survive long enough to bond adequately with you. That's why it's illegal that way."

The tourists perked up, excited. Some had come to buy. Their clueless enthusiasm pained me, like it always had.

"How many do you have today?" a larger, balding man asked in broken English.

"I am not allowed to tell you until the end of the tour. If I did, there would be a mass stampede. As you know, we have to sell them every day. They go quickly. The first tourist groups of the day are the ones who go home with the Lucent Sylphs." The guide explained things honestly, but her words implied a scarce supply.

Antsy and over-eager, the tourists began crowding her for more information, a couple of them breaking away from the group and making a run for it. She called after them, distracted, "I don't think I was supposed to say that! I'm new and I messed up! Wait!"

I took my opportunity to duck down the ladder. Crouching on a small platform below the rungs, away from my group, yet also out of view of the cameras, I opened my bag. Gingerly lifting out the heavy canister, I pressed the face of the chip taped securely to the inside. I could hear my words begin, soft and rhythmic, reverberating gently off of the canister walls.

Nissa was too bright, and her heart was too large. She had been more luminescent than ever – since the bus.

"Will leaving me bring your heart back down in size?" I asked, worried.

"It might. But, Lucas…" she began.

"We don't have much time!" I reminded her. "Any moment now they will realize I'm not in the group. You need to get inside and brace yourself. I will seal it up, and then I only have to run and throw you into the rippling air before I'm caught."

"What will happen to you?" she asked. She sounded concerned.

"Probably a slap on the wrist. I'm sure I'm not the first person who attempted to throw something into the portal. I don't think anyone's made it, though."

"That is not true," she whispered. Her voice was too soft. Her veins bulged inside of her glass body.

"What isn't true?" I lowered my voice. "Someone else made it through?"

"No. That you will only get a 'slap on the wrist.' You will be in serious trouble."

I felt frustration rising, and I hoped it helped ease her throbbing heart. "I always knew that! I knew what I was getting into. It's worth it to me!" I held her to my shoulder, hugging her as gently as I could. "You're going to make it, Nissa!"

She was so hot to the touch. Her body felt like it could burn my hand. I lowered her quickly into the canister. I said nothing more, as there was nothing more to say. A drawn-out goodbye would endanger her further. Only a few more minutes, and then the devastation of our separation should shrink her heart back to its normal s ze, like a deflated balloon. I just hoped that the recording would bolster her strength.

She looked at me, from inside of the canister, and cocked her head at the sound of my recorded voice. I was saying something about, *You are the most precious, most beautiful being I have ever known, and my heart beats only for you.*

I flushed. "I recorded it that day I forced you to go outside and wait. Couldn't have you around to hear it, or it would have killed you for sure. Now, hurry!"

She looked at me, for an instant, and I panicked. I tried to close it up hurriedly so that I could fling it from me as quickly as possible. Her hand reached up and stopped the lid, little cracks forming on her fingers.

"No, you can't…" I babbled, terror filling my vision.

She was red all over, and the cracks spread down her arm. Her whole body pulsed like she was a single heart. If her mouth and eyes could smile, they did then.

"Unfortunately, you could not prevent this," she said, her voice as smooth and soft as trickling water. "I would have died in the portal regardless without the source of your emotion, but I was hoping to survive until you sent me away. Yet, the very act of you sacrificing so much for me is overwhelming me sooner than I expected."

"That's not possible!" I roared, tears flooding my eyes.

"You Love me enough to send me away."

"I should've kept you then! Why didn't you tell me it would kill you?"

She lowered her cracked hand. The fissures were forming all over her body. "I wanted you to assume you

180

had succeeded in sending me home. Keeping me would have killed me as well, eventually. Your Love is vast."

I sobbed and tried to clear my eyes so that I could see her. Tears should not blur my last view of her. "You can still go! Don't talk anymore! You're still alive! I'm throwing you away now! I'm getting rid of you! I hate you! Don't you see?"

While my mouth spit out the vile words, my heart rang true. I could not lie to a Lucent Sylph.

Nissa's eyes were bathed in an inner light, soft and deep. "Instead of dying in private, I dare to confront you now. Let me speak while I still am able. While I have this chance.

"Lucas, I have lived the happiest and best of lives. I have learned to intensely Love you, and to be Loved in return."

"I will throw you away now!" I threatened, shouting, not worrying if anyone heard and stopped me.

She blocked the lid once more, her grasp strong, mine weak with anguish. "I do not want you to remain unchanged by what you have been through. What I'm about to leave you is my Love melted down. *Do* something with it. You have the most beautiful heart of any human I have heard tale of. Do not hide it away. Do not be afraid to Love. God is Love. Love like He Loves."

My weeping was loud and insistent when it happened. With a sound like breaking glass, Nissa shattered into a million pieces, each piece becoming sparkling, shimmery dust. The dust rained down on the insides of the canister, some floating out to rest on my nose and coat my hair. It sparkled, sang, and was full of multiple colors. It smelled of roses. It had a melody and a harmony that blended for an instant and was gone. It was the most beautiful display of art that I had ever seen.

But she was gone.

I love you. I love you more than my own life, my voice was intoning through the micronano chip. I silenced it. Then held the glittery substance against my face and cried.

Two years later, with the help of my schoolteachers and some city leaders, I officially opened the first counseling center for grieving former owners of Lucent Sylphs. I discovered that there were many people suffering like myself, needing community and hope. Needing closure and forgiveness. Many who felt like murderers for their hand in killing the beings they had grown to adore. Many with a story of pain and hopelessness.

I found that I had a gift of comfort and of sympathy. This was something I wanted to do for the rest of my life.

We can't stop the Lucent Sylphs from coming in droves to our world. We also can't stop them from being bought or sold. And we can't stop them from dying.

But we can provide healing and care for those who had attempted to own one, who had peeked into the heart of these magnificent creatures. Who had felt the devotion and loyalty, grace and affection they freely gave without care of their life.

Together, we can be Love for each other.

Reviews help authors! Think about leaving an honest review for this story on Amazon.

Connect with RJ Conte:

Facebook:

https://www.facebook.com/BlondeRJConte/

Twitter: @BlondeRJConte

Website: https://blonderj.wordpress.com

Thank you!

65805998R00111

Made in the USA
Middletown, DE
05 March 2018